# "It's That Time Of The Month,"

Rebecca blurted out. Meaning, of course, that she wasn't pregnant. She risked a glance at Zach and found his expression as grim-lipped as she expected. She bit back an apology. It wasn't for want of trying that she wasn't pregnant. She and Zach made love at least once a day and sometimes twice. She looked forward to those interludes, because otherwise, Zach avoided her company.

She was running out of time—time to either get pregnant or somehow make her new husband fall in love with her.

Dear Reader,

Here at Desire, hot summer months mean even *hotter* reading, beginning with Joan Johnston's *The Disobedient Bride*, the next addition to her fabulous Children of Hawk's Way series—*and* July's *Man of the Month*.

Next up is *Falcon's Lair*, a sizzling love story by Sara Orwig, an author many of you already know—although she's new to Desire. And if you like family stories, don't miss Christine Rimmer's unforgettable *Cat's Cradle* or Caroline Cross's delightful *Operation Mommy*.

A book from award winner Helen R. Myers is always a treat, so I'm glad we have *The Rebel and the Hero* this month. And Diana Mars's many fans will be thrilled with *Mixed-up Matrimony*. If you like humor, you'll like this engaging—and *very* sensuous—love story.

Next month, there is much more to look forward to, including *The Wilde Bunch*, a *Man of the Month* by Barbara Boswell, and *Heart of the Hunter*, the first book in a new series by BJ James.

As always, your opinions are important to me. So continue to let me know what you like about Silhouette Desire!

Sincerely,

Lucia Macro
Senior Editor

---

Please address questions and book requests to:
Silhouette Reader Service
U.S.: 3010 Walden Ave., P.O. Box 1325, Buffalo, NY 14269
Canadian: P.O. Box 609, Fort Erie, Ont. L2A 5X3

# *Joan Johnston*
## THE DISOBEDIENT BRIDE

SILHOUETTE *Desire®*
Published by Silhouette Books
America's Publisher of Contemporary Romance

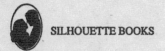

SILHOUETTE BOOKS

ISBN 0-373-05937-X

THE DISOBEDIENT BRIDE

## JOAN JOHNSTON

started reading romances to escape the stress of being an attorney with a major national law firm. She soon discovered that writing romances was a lot more fun than writing legal bond indentures. Since then, she has published a number of historical and contemporary category romances. In addition to being an author, Joan is the mother of two children. In her spare time, she enjoys sailing, horseback riding and camping.

This book is dedicated to my editor,
Melissa Senate, who knows when to push
and when to have patience.
Thanks, Mel.

# Prologue

---

"Something wrong, Miss Littlewolf?"

Rebecca surreptitiously wiped the tears from her cheeks and glanced up into warm brown eyes that were caught in a tangled web of crow's-feet. "I'm fine, Mrs. Fortunata. Just a little tired, I guess."

She and the short, rotund Italian woman had become friends because they both worked the graveyard shift at Children's Hospital. Mrs. Fortunata mopped and buffed the floors every night. Rebecca was a nurse for children with cancer.

The hospital cafeteria was nearly deserted. Rebecca's shift had ended a half hour ago, but she didn't have the will to get up and go home.

"You don't fool me," Mrs. Fortunata said. "Eyes red like that, you got a cold or you got a problem. Which is it?"

"Timmy Carstairs died tonight."

"You shouldn't let yourself care so much," Mrs. Fortunata gently chided.

"I know." A ragged sigh escaped. "I try to figure out which ones will make it, and which ones won't." Rebecca paused to swallow the huge lump in her throat. "I thought Timmy was going to be one of the lucky ones. He sure had me fooled." She tried to smile, but her lips wobbled dangerously.

Mrs. Fortunata shoved her mop into the nearby pail and wedged herself into the booth beside Rebecca. She took Rebecca's hand in hers and patted it. "Nice young thing like you oughta be headed home to a husband and kids of her own."

Rebecca tried for the smile again. And failed again. It was Mrs. Fortunata's life ambition to see her married and pregnant. Preferably in that order. "Maybe someday."

Mrs. Fortunata snorted. "You been sayin' that the whole two years I've known you. Why don't I ever see you with some nice young man? Ever since you kissed that Marty What's-his-name goodbye, you've been alone. You got something against men these days?"

This time Rebecca managed the smile. "No. I like men just fine."

"You haven't met the right man yet, is that it?"

Rebecca retrieved her hand and took a sip of lukewarm coffee to keep from having to answer. She had met the right man years ago. But she hadn't been the right woman for him.

"How're you gonna fill up your life," Mrs. Fortunata demanded, with flourishing gestures to emphasize her point, "if you don't find yourself a husband and have yourself some children?"

"I'd like to run a summer camp for kids with cancer," Rebecca replied. "If I could just figure out a way to finance it." The kids who were in remission needed a place where they could go and just be kids, but they often had special needs that couldn't be met by a regular camp experience. "It's probably never going to happen, but I can always dream."

"Everybody dreams. Only, you gotta do something to make those dreams come true. Me, I wanta quit moppin' floors someday."

"Why, Mrs. Fortunata, I thought you liked mopping floors," Rebecca teased.

"Tell you what. You get a camp for kids, you hire me to work for you. I quit moppin' floors like that." Mrs. Fortunata snapped two arthritic fingers together, or tried to. She gave up and made a flamboyant gesture that said it all without the snap.

"Meanwhile, you look here." Mrs. Fortunata reached into a pocket in the huge set of white overalls she wore and produced a ragged newspaper. She shoved it in front of Rebecca. "You need a husband. Here's a man who wants a wife. You give him a call. What do you say?"

Rebecca stared at the advertisement in the personals section of the Dallas newspaper.

### WIFE WANTED

Texas rancher seeks honest, responsible, compliant woman for wife. Must be capable of bearing children. Contact Zachary Whitelaw, Hawk's Pride, or phone 555-6748.

Her eyes went wide with disbelief. "I know this man!"

"You do?"

Rebecca nodded excitedly. "My father was foreman of his ranch. I lived at Hawk's Pride from the time I was thirteen until I turned seventeen."

"Why'd you leave?"

"My dad died from a heart attack, and I used the life insurance settlement to go to college. There was no reason to go back."

"Now there is. You see this man. You tell him you want to be his wife."

"I can't do that."

"Why not?"

"He's already told me to get lost once. I don't need to be told a second time that I'm not wanted."

"Aha! So he's the reason you don't like other men!"

"I never said—"

"I see what you don't say," Mrs. Fortunata said. "You loved him. Fine. Don't let him get away this time."

"Mrs. Fortunata—"

"No excuses. You go see this man. You tell him you'd make a good wife."

"Look at the date on this paper," Rebecca said in desperation. "It's three weeks old. He's probably already found a wife."

"And maybe not."

"I just couldn't."

"What're you waiting for? You're gonna be an old lady all alone like me, you don't do something quick."

Rebecca laughed. "You were married for forty years before Mr. Fortunata died. You've got ten grandchildren!"

"My kids have moved all over the country. I don't see all those grandbabies so much as I'd like anymore. I miss them. You keep foolin' around, you won't even have grandbabies to miss!"

Rebecca laughed again. "All right. I give up. I'll go see him."

But it wasn't going to do any good. Zach Whitelaw had already told her to stay the hell out of his way. Of course, she had only been a kid of seventeen at the time.

Maybe he would be willing to take a second look at a mature woman of twenty-three.

# One

---

"**I** saw your advertisement for a wife. I've come to apply for the job."

Zach Whitelaw stared in astonishment at the woman dressed in a white T-shirt, jeans and boots on the other side of the screen door. "Becky? Is that you?" His lips slowly curled with amusement. He shoved the door open and said, "Come on in, kid."

"I'm not a—"

"Kid," he finished as he tugged on the waist-length black hair that had fallen over her shoulder. His grin broadened as he looked her over from head to toe. Their eyes met and his face sobered. "It's been a long time."

"Six years."

"Surely not that long?"

Rebecca nodded. She stood mute beneath Zach's perusal, but couldn't prevent the flush that turned skin that was a warm honey color—thanks to her Comanche forebears—a deeper hue.

"Nope. You're definitely not a kid anymore," he said at last. "What have you been doing with yourself?"

"I'm a nurse at Children's Hospital in Dallas."

"Figures," he said with a grin. "Last time I saw you a ragged-eared mutt was stumping along behind you on a splint you'd rigged up for his broken leg. Whatever happened to that mutt, anyway?"

"That 'mutt' is named Pepper," she said archly, "and I left him with friends in Dallas."

"Are you still rescuing every helpless critter that crosses your path?"

"I've had to cut back some," she conceded with a smile. "There's not much extra space in a one-bedroom condo."

"You had quite a collection of the walking wounded when you lived here with your dad." He chuckled. "Everything from a skunk to a snake."

"I could never stand to see anything in pain," she said without apology. "It's a major failing of mine."

"Must make it hard to work with sick kids," he said.

Oh, how perceptive he was. He always had been.

"Sometimes it is hard." More than sometimes, but she hadn't come to Zach for a shoulder to cry on.

Rebecca felt caught in the warp of time, unable to move in or out of the doorway. She had fallen madly in love with Zach at the age of thirteen. She had fantasized what it would be like to be kissed by him, to be held in his strong arms. She had hinted at what a good kisser she might become, if only she had someone to practice on. He had ignored the fumbling adolescent signals she had sent out and treated her like a bratty younger sister, letting her work with him. With amazing patience, he had taught her everything there was to know about ranching. But not a blamed thing about kissing.

Unfortunately, long before she was old enough to catch Zach's eye, he had fallen in love with another—much older—woman of twenty-two. She had thought she would die when Zach told her he planned to marry Cynthia Kenyon.

"You can't get married!" she had cried. "You can't!"

"Look, kid—"

"I'm not a kid, I'm a woman!"

He had laughed at her. Laughed! "Look, kid—"

"Don't call me that!"

"But you are a kid," he said gently. "Sweet sixteen and never been kissed. Wait a few years. Some man will come along and fall head over heels for you."

She had stared at him in horror. It dawned on her suddenly that he wasn't going to wait for her to grow up. He was going to marry Cynthia Kenyon and be lost to her forever.

"You're so stupid," she had gibed. "You don't know anything!" She had run then, searching for a place to hide, a place where she could nurse her pain alone.

Hours later, her father had found her in the loft of the barn. Her fondest memory of her father was the way he had comforted her that day. He had settled on his knees in the straw, folded her into his arms and held her while she cried, her body heaving with great wrenching sobs of terrible grief. When her body was exhausted, and she could cry no more, he had gently wiped away the tears with his bandanna.

"I know you think this is the end of the world," he said. "But someday you'll grow up and fall in love, and you'll realize this was just a childhood infatuation."

She had believed him. Or tried to believe him. But his words hadn't been much comfort to a vulnerable girl with a broken heart.

The next time she saw Zach, she had managed to stutter, "I w-wish you and Cynthia a l-lifetime of l-love and happiness."

He had put a brotherly arm around her shoulder. "That means a lot to me, kid." Then he had cuffed her chin playfully with his knuckles and let her go.

She hadn't gone near him for a whole week. Eventually, she had decided she might as well enjoy his company while she could. But things were never quite the same between them after that. She caught him staring at her more than once with an odd look in his eyes that made her uncomfortable.

It had been a sore test for her immortal soul when, two days before the wedding, Cynthia had been killed in a plane crash. Somehow she had managed to express the appropriate sympathy, but Zach had been inconsolable. She had held on to the hope, slight though it was, that he might turn to her in his grief.

He had not.

In all these years, and despite her father's promise that Zach would become a part of her past, she had never fallen out of love with him. She had dated occasionally and had even been engaged once. But Zach Whitelaw had been the standard by which she had measured all other men. She had backed out of her engagement because she had realized she was being unfair to Marty What's-his-name, as Mrs. Fortunata referred to him, by constantly comparing him unfavorably to Zach.

"Are you coming in, or not?" Zach asked.

"I'm coming in." She was momentarily shadowed by Zach's over-six-foot height as she stepped inside the kitchen of his adobe ranch house. He hissed in a breath as the tips of her breasts brushed against his shirt. They froze momentarily at the shocking contact. Zach reached out and took her shoulders in a tight grasp to separate their bodies. Nevertheless, a frisson of electricity continued to arc between them.

The attraction was there. It had been there since *the incident* between them when she was seventeen. At least on her side. She had no idea what Zach felt. It was because of *the incident* that she had kept her distance all these years.

"Those tactics won't work any better this time than they did the last," he said abruptly.

She looked up and found herself captured by eyes that were dark and dangerous. "I didn't mean to brush against you, Zach. It was an accident."

"Like the last time was an accident?"

He hadn't forgotten *the incident* any more than she had.

It had happened six years ago, before she left for college, but a full year after Cynthia's death. Zach had become a morose and moody man. She had wanted him to turn to her, to see her as the woman who could replace Cynthia in his mind and his heart. She had wanted him to marry her so they could be together forever. But he still didn't see her as a woman. So she had picked her moment and purposely tripped and fallen against him in the barn.

Their bodies had come into close, hard contact. She had reveled in his harsh intake of breath as her breasts pillowed against his chest. She vividly remembered the swirling dust motes caught in a golden shaft of sunlight, the pungent smells of hay and manure.

His hands had closed around her waist as though to push her away, yet he hadn't. Their faces had been close enough that she could feel his warm, damp breath against her cheek. But she had been the one who had to lift her lips to his.

She had been surprised by their softness. And disappointed when he jerked his face away. He had released her quickly and exhaled with a short huff. She had seen the evidence of his response to her in the tight fit of his jeans and smiled up at him. Her smile had faded when he failed to return it.

The look on his face had been terrible to see. His lips had flattened, and his eyes went cold. His hands balled into white-knuckled fists at his sides.

"Don't ever do that again," he said.

"Do what?" she asked with feigned innocence.

"Look, little girl," he said in a steely voice. "Don't play the tease unless you want to end up flat on your back with me on top of you."

She had flushed with embarrassment at such frank speaking. And tried again to deny her guilt. "I wasn't—"

"I like you, kid," he said quietly. "But I'm no good for you. Stay away from me."

She wrinkled her nose. "I'm not a—"

"Kid? You're seventeen. I'm thirty. Give yourself some time to grow up. Then find a man who can love you, and settle down and have some kids of your own."

"But you're the man I want!" she blurted.

His lips tilted on one side in a bittersweet smile. "I'll never love another woman, kid." His dark eyes turned merciless. "Just stay the hell away from me."

Seeing the same warning look in his eyes now as she had seen that long ago day, Rebecca put some distance between herself and Zach. At the sink she turned to face him again. "Why are you advertising for a wife, Zach? I would think you could have any woman you wanted just by asking."

"Actually, I don't want a wife."

"What?"

"I need a woman to be the mother of my children. I advertised for a wife so there'll be no misunderstanding that it's purely a business arrangement. Still want to apply for the job?"

Rebecca swallowed hard. "I see. That puts a new light on things." She had thought he was finally over Cynthia, but apparently not.

However, if this was the way he intended to acquire a wife, she would have to do her best to cope with the situation. She met all his qualifications. Or almost all. She was honest and responsible and would love having Zach's children. She had dismissed the *compliant* part of the ad. Zach should have known better than to write something like that in this day and age. But the "business arrangement" he had described raised questions in her mind.

"What about love?" Rebecca asked.

"What about it?"

"Don't you want a wife who'll love you?"

"It isn't necessary. In fact, it would be a nuisance, since I don't expect to love her back."

Rebecca had always fantasized that someday Zach would fall in love with her, and they would marry and live happily ever after. It was the stuff fairy tales were made of.

Zach had just announced he had no intention of falling in love with her or any other woman. Her brow furrowed in thought. He wasn't offering much, but it would take a harder man than the Zach Whitelaw she knew to resist all the love she planned to heap on him.

She gave him a brilliant smile and said, "I'm your woman, Zach. I'd be perfect for the job."

Zach laughed aloud. "Forget it, kid." He grabbed a bar stool from the center island, turned it around and straddled it. He crossed his arms on the stool's wooden back and grinned. "My advertisement was quite specific. You're not exactly what I had in mind."

"But, I—"

"Zach, there's another applicant at the front door who says—" The petite, dark-eyed, dark-haired woman stopped in her tracks at the kitchen door. "Becky! I didn't know you were here."

Rebecca gave Zach's younger sister a friendly smile. "Hi, Callen. You're looking great. I understand you're a new mother." She had caught up on all the local gossip at the Stanton Hotel in town where she was staying.

Callen laid her hands on her nearly flat abdomen. "I didn't know it showed."

Rebecca gave her a quizzical look. "I was talking about the twins, Kayla and Karen."

"Then you don't know about this one?"

"This one?"

She grinned. "Sam and I are expecting another child in six and a half months. This baby was a surprise with the twins only a year old, but it's very welcome."

"How is Sam holding up?" Rebecca asked.

"Sam's still in shock," Callen replied with a sheepish look. "It's a nice kind of shock, because we want a large family. But tell me about you. Are you just visiting, or are you here to stay?"

Rebecca shot a quick glance in Zach's direction. "That depends on Zach. I saw his advertisement for a wife, and I've come to apply for the job."

"Not you, too!" Callen said in disgust. "For the record, I disapprove of this whole business. Mom and Daddy aren't too keen on it, either. A man ought to marry because he's in love, not because he's decided it's time he had an heir and needs an appropriate brood mare. I can't believe you'd put yourself in the running. As much as I love my brother, he'd be hell to live with. And given his attitude toward women, he'll make a terrible husband."

"I think he'd be fine husband material, assuming he got the right wife." Rebecca glanced quickly at Zach, at the lock of thick, black hair that had fallen on his brow, at the dark, inscrutable eyes in his finely chiseled face, at the high, wide cheekbones, and his straight nose and strong chin. It was an arresting face, and Rebecca had to force her eyes away from Zach and back to his sister.

Callen snorted and rolled her eyes. "You don't know my brother like I do. He's an arrogant, chauvinistic Neanderthal who hasn't been in a real relationship with a woman since Cynthia—"

Callen cut herself off. Apparently, even so many years after her death, Cynthia was a taboo subject. "I can't imagine what woman would want to attach herself to Zach for life!"

"Lucky for me I don't require a recommendation from you," Zach said with a lazy grin.

"Omigosh! I almost forgot. There's a woman in the living room who wants an interview, Zach. Is she number fourteen or fifteen?"

"Seventeen, actually."

Rebecca was amazed and appalled at the number of women Zach had already rejected, but also encouraged. He must not be as ready to leap into marriage with a stranger as he professed.

Zach rose. "Duty calls."

"May I come along?" Rebecca asked.

"Why not?"

"I'm coming, too," Callen said. "I don't want to miss this," she said in an aside to Rebecca. "Wait until you see the kind of woman that's been replying to Zach's ad."

Rebecca wasn't sure what she was expecting, maybe a poor, plain, uneducated woman, who couldn't get a husband any other way. That would explain all those rejected applicants.

The woman sitting on Zach's saddle-brown leather couch was absolutely beautiful, self-assured, sophisticated and utterly relaxed. Rebecca felt her heart sink. No wonder Zach had laughed when she announced herself as an applicant for the position of wife. She was pretty and poised, but she just wasn't in the same ballpark as the beauty in Zach's living room. If this was her competition, she had her work cut out for her. She dropped into a pine rocker across from the couch and waited for the show to start.

"Hello," the woman said in a husky voice.

She even sounded sexy, Rebecca thought with dismay.

"I'm Zach Whitelaw," Zach said.

Rebecca didn't like the wolfish smile on his face as he ogled the woman.

The woman reached out a hand, which Zach took as he sat beside her on the couch.

"I'm Harriet Thomas."

The woman never took her eyes off Zach, and he seemed equally entranced. Rebecca cleared her throat loudly.

"I'm Rebecca Littlewolf."

Harriet never even glanced at her. Instead she said to Zach, "What would you like to know about me?"

"Zach's going to marry me," Rebecca said.

A flash of annoyance crossed Harriet's face. "I didn't know the position was filled."

"It's not," Zach said. "Cut it out, kid."

Rebecca wasn't intimidated by Zach's scowl. She had seen it plenty of times as a teenager, and the worst that had ever resulted was a severe tongue-lashing. "You do realize that Zach wants *lots* of children."

Harriet arched a finely tweezed brow. She turned to Zach, awaiting his response.

"That's true," Zach admitted.

"How many?" the woman asked.

"Three for sure, maybe four."

"I see." Harriet pursed her lips in a way that wasn't at all flattering. She stood abruptly and turned to face Rebecca. "He's all yours."

"I'll show Ms. Thomas out," Callen said with a wink at Rebecca.

"I can find my own way out."

Callen gestured toward the front door. When it had closed behind the woman, she turned back to the tension-filled room. "Oh, how I wish I could stay and hear the denouement in this little drama! But I've got a doctor's appointment, and if I don't leave right now I'm going to be terribly late. It was nice to see you, Becky," she said as she grabbed her car keys and headed for the door. "Good luck with my brother. You're going to need it!"

A moment later Rebecca found herself trapped in the rocker as Zach wrapped his powerful hands around each of the arms and leaned over to put his nose an inch from hers.

"This isn't a game to me, kid," he said in a feral voice. "I need a wife. And I intend to find one."

Rebecca swallowed over the sudden lump in her throat. "You've found her. I'm right here." She looked up at him, her heart pounding crazily, careful not to let the love she felt show in her eyes. Zach didn't want or expect love from a wife.

Zach suddenly stood and shoved all ten fingers through his hair. "It would never work."

Rebecca was startled by his response, which suggested he might have considered the idea. She leapt from the rocker and put herself directly in front of him, hands on hips, chin up, shoulders squared in a fighting stance. "Why wouldn't it work? Actually, if you think about it, I'm the perfect woman for the job. I know everything there is to know about a working ranch—you taught me yourself—and I'm familiar with every inch of Hawk's Pride. You know I'm honest and responsible." She flushed and said, "And I can provide a doctor's report to ensure I'm capable of having children."

She purposely didn't mention the *compliant* part, hoping he would forget about it. She took a deep breath and continued. "And I, more than any other applicant, know exactly why you don't want or expect love to be a part of the bargain." Meaning, she knew how much he had loved Cynthia.

When he didn't immediately refuse her, she let herself hope. When his teeth clenched, when the muscle in his jaw began to work, she felt a desperate sense of loss.

"Zach, just think about it."

"No, kid. And that's my final word on the subject."

He took one step before she managed to block his path with her body. "I refuse to accept that answer."

Zach grimaced. "That is exactly why you'd make me a terrible wife. There's not a *compliant* bone in your body."

"At least you know what you'd be getting," Rebecca argued. "You know me, Zach. You like me. Isn't that important?"

"Why do you want to marry me?" Zach demanded. "You've got your whole life ahead of you. What would you get out of an arrangement like this?"

Rebecca managed to keep herself from blurting *You!* Any hint of love would be the death knell to whatever hope she had of marrying Zach. She searched frantically for some reason Zach would accept and believe. And hit on the perfect response.

"Ever since I started working at Children's Hospital I've dreamed of starting a summer camp for kids with cancer. I could never afford that sort of thing on my own. If I were your wife, I could realize my dream here at Hawk's Pride."

His lip curled. "I see. So it's my money you find attractive."

"Well, you're not bad-looking, either," she quipped. One look at his face, and she knew she had better do some fast talking.

"The camp really is a wonderful idea, Zach." Her voice filled with enthusiasm as she warmed to her subject. "Hawk's Pride would be a perfect place to bring kids who've never seen a horse or a steer. We could teach them to ride horseback, or take them for rides in a hay wagon. It would be so good for them. If only you could see how hard they work just to stay alive, never mind to get well, you'd realize what a perfect reward a week at a working ranch would be."

Zach's eyes narrowed, as though to assess the truth of what she had said. He tucked his thumbs in his back pockets. "I suppose I would finance this camp of yours."

Rebecca nodded.

"How would you manage the four kids I want and a camp, too?"

"I'd hire good help."

"For the camp... or the kids?" Zach asked cynically.

"I'd be a good mother, Zach," Rebecca said seriously. "I lost my mother when I was born, so I know how much a child needs one. I'd give your—

our—children all the love they could ever want or
need."

Zach shook his head. "I don't know, Becky. I have
to admit that camp idea sounds good. I've got a
niece, Susannah—my brother Falcon's stepdaughter—who has leukemia. She'd love to go to a camp
like the one you want to start. But it would be a lot
of work."

Rebecca took great heart from the fact he hadn't
called her *kid*. "I can handle it, Zach. Believe me,
I'm the woman you're looking for. Admit it. I'm
perfect for the job."

He eyed her suspiciously. "I haven't forgotten
what you said when you were seventeen."

Rebecca couldn't keep the stricken look off her
face. If she couldn't disabuse him of the notion that
she still loved him after all these years, she might lose
everything. She managed to put a ladle of scorn in
her voice. "I hope you're not going to hold the foolish words of an adolescent against me. I might have
been infatuated with you at seventeen, but I've
grown up a lot since then."

"I've noticed," he said. "And I can't say I'm not
attracted. I am." He took the steps necessary to close
the distance between them. "I'd forgotten how green
your eyes are, like spring grass. And I love the feel of
your hair," he said as he fingered a handful of the
silky strands.

"I'm attracted to you, too, Zach. In a physical
way," she corrected hastily.

Rebecca laid a tentative hand on Zach's chest, near his heart. She could feel the hard muscle even through his Western shirt. Her hand slid up his chest and curled around his nape into untrimmed hair that was soft and thick.

She saw what was going to happen, waited for it, wanted it. He was going to kiss her. He watched her with dark, unfathomable eyes, until he was so close she was forced to lower her lids. He paused, a breath away, then touched his lips to hers.

Goose bumps popped up on her arms, and her knees buckled. Fortunately he caught her with an arm around her waist and pulled her close.

And deepened the kiss.

His tongue was hot and wet and came slow and deep into her mouth. She made an animal sound low in her throat and heard an answering growl from him. His arm tightened around her waist, and he cupped her behind and lifted her enough to fit their bodies intimately together.

She arched toward him, enthralled by his need for her. Her arms clung to his shoulders, while her mouth clung to his.

Suddenly she was standing by herself, chest heaving, legs wobbling, hands trembling. She stared, dazed, at Zach, who had backed up a good three feet from her.

"Well, I guess that's settled," he said.

"What's settled?"

"We'd be all right together in bed."

"Oh."

He tunneled splayed fingers into his hair. "I don't know, kid. This is so incredible. When I put that ad in the paper, I never imagined that someone I knew would answer it. I have to think about this."

Rebecca knew that if she gave Zach time to think, he would come up with a dozen excuses to reject her. "You won't find a better candidate than me, Zach. You'll be getting exactly what you want—a wife who'll marry you without expecting love and who'll give you children—without having to waste any more time looking. You have the added advantage of marrying someone you know, someone your family will accept and approve."

She saw Zach's eyes widen as he realized the truth of her pronouncement. According to Callen, Zach's parents disapproved of his method of choosing a wife. Marrying Rebecca Littlewolf, someone they knew, was bound to lessen their concern.

"Don't think too long, Zach. I have to return to Dallas in a couple of days."

"Then maybe I'd better make this decision right now."

Rebecca felt her heart begin to thud in her chest. Surely Zach could hear it, surely he knew how much she wanted to be his wife, and not at all for the reason she had told him.

"There are a few things we need to get straight first."

"Such as?"

"Don't delude yourself into thinking I'll fall in love with you. I won't. I'll never love another woman. Not after Cynthia."

Rebecca felt her stomach roll. "All right. What else?"

"I'm marrying because I want children. But I'm a man, and I have needs that I'll expect my wife to satisfy."

Goose bumps prickled her flesh at the thought of lying beneath him...above him...beside him in bed. "I'll be glad to satisfy those needs, presuming I'm the only woman who'll enjoy those pleasures," she said, answering his demand for sexual services with her demand for fidelity. "Anything else?"

"I'll expect you to devote yourself to the children first and foremost. In exchange, I'll see to it you get the financing and whatever other help you need for that camp you want for sick kids."

"Agreed."

"One more thing. If you're not pregnant a year from now, we get a divorce. After all, what I want is children, not a barren wife."

She sucked in a harsh breath, appalled at this unforeseen condition. "That's a cold-blooded thing to say."

He shrugged. "Take it or leave it."

For the first time since she had fallen in love with him at thirteen, Rebecca wondered if she was mistaken about Zach. The man she had found lovable could never have been so ruthless. Clearly this man was. What if she couldn't make him love her? What if Zach truly had become a heartless man? What if she spent the next year of her life falling deeper and deeper in love with him and then failed to become pregnant? Were the rewards to be had from marrying Zach Whitelaw worth the risks?

"If we divorce, I continue to run the summer camp here at Hawk's Pride, and you continue to fund it. I want that in writing," Rebecca said.

"No demand for alimony?"

Rebecca shook her head. "I told you what I want from this marriage." *Or almost all of what I want.*

"Given everything I've just said, do you still want to marry me?" he asked.

"I do."

It wasn't until Zach heaved a sigh of relief that Rebecca realized he hadn't been at all certain of her response. And that he seemed pleased by it. The grin that appeared moments later confirmed his feelings. "I guess we have a deal."

"How soon do you want to have the wedding?" Rebecca asked.

"Tomorrow. We can get Judge Smithers to officiate."

"No."

"There you go again, disagreeing with me," Zach said. "What am I going to do with you, kid?"

He gave her that same playful cuff he had administered when she was a girl of seventeen. She looked into his eyes, wondering what he saw when he looked at her. She wasn't the young girl who had left Hawk's Pride six years ago. She had a woman's needs, a woman's dreams and desires. She wanted much more than Zach seemed to be offering.

She had a moment's qualm, but fought it down. She wasn't going to lose the brass ring just because she hadn't reached for it.

"I have to give at least two weeks' notice at the hospital, Zach."

"All right, two weeks. Not a day more."

"Deal," Rebecca said, extending her hand.

Zach took it and pulled her close. "I'd rather seal our bargain this way," he said as his mouth claimed hers.

She felt his need and answered with her own. His strong arms, the ones she had dreamed about for so many years, closed around her, and he lifted her enough so that she felt his sure and certain arousal. His breathing roughened, and she heard a guttural sound of triumph issue from his throat.

It was going to be a rare match of wills, all right. Rebecca was gambling that she could tame the savage beast. She only hoped he didn't devour her before she got the chance.

# Two

Zach wanted a woman. It wasn't the first time he had stared at the bedroom ceiling and denied his body's raging need. But tonight the object of his desire had a face and a name.

Rebecca Littlewolf.

It wasn't a bad thing to physically desire one's future bride, Zach thought. But he was surprised by the intensity of his need and at his inability to banish the tantalizing image of her green eyes and flowing black hair from his mind. He could imagine her eyes, lambent with passion, feel her silky hair draped over his naked torso.

Zach rose and paced restlessly into the living room, where a picture window overlooked the vast acres of Hawk's Pride. It was nearly dawn, and he could see the silhouette of rocky outcroppings that marked the entrance to a deep canyon on his property. He could see a windmill flying in the Texas wind and cattle feeding on the prairie grass.

On his twenty-first birthday, his father had given him this piece of property carved out of land that had been in the Whitelaw family for generations. He had looked forward to marrying and raising a family who would bring love and laughter into his life. That was all before Cynthia Kenyon.

Cynthia had been his first love and, filled with tales of his parents' romance told by the fireplace on long winter nights in his youth, he had fallen hard. She had moved in with him as soon as they were engaged. Two days before their wedding, he had discovered Cynthia in his bed with another man.

He had knocked the man unconscious with one blow; it had taken every ounce of self-control he had to keep from hitting her. He had carefully uncurled his knotted fists and shoved his thumbs into the back pockets of his jeans.

"Get out, Cynthia, and take that carcass on the floor with you."

"It didn't mean anything, Zach. He works for a New York modeling agency. He's going to offer me a contract. It has nothing to do with us."

It had amazed him that she could so cavalierly share her body with another man. And that she expected him not to care. "It means something to me," he said. "Get out, Cynthia. And don't come back."

"Don't do this, Zach," she pleaded. Big tears welled in her eyes and spilled onto her cheeks. "I love you. I made a mistake. Please, forgive me."

"Some things are unforgivable."

"I'm pregnant, Zach."

"With whose kid?"

He would never forget the look on her face, a mixture of confusion and fear.

"It's yours, Zach."

He didn't believe her. What man would have under the circumstances? She wasn't pregnant, or if she was, it wasn't his kid. He felt like a fool and an idiot. He had trusted her, and she had betrayed him. He didn't think there was any way he could ever forget the sight of her flesh joined to that of another man in his bed. He felt physically ill.

"Get out, Cynthia. And don't come back."

"All right, Zach, I'm going, but you'll be sorry someday. This is your baby I'm carrying, and I'll prove it. Then you'll pay. Will you ever pay!"

Cynthia and her lover had boarded a private plane headed for New York. It crashed shortly after takeoff, killing everyone on board.

Zach had asked the coroner whether Cynthia was pregnant.

"I'm afraid so, son," the man had replied. "I'm truly very sorry."

The guilt he felt over Cynthia's death had been bad enough. It didn't approach the horror he experienced at knowing a child—his child?—had died with her. There was no way he could ask for any kind of test to prove things one way or the other without revealing his doubt. So he grieved the baby's death. But he had always wondered whether she had made a fool of him in the end by making him mourn some other man's child.

It had been especially painful to see the tears in his mother's eyes, the haggard look on his father's face, when they heard the news of the death of their unborn grandchild. He had been too hurt, too humiliated, to admit to his family the possibility that the child wasn't his. Maybe it had been his. He would have to live with that uncertainty the rest of his life.

It had been almost impossible to graciously accept the sympathy offered to him on the death of his bride only two days before their wedding. Nobody knew of Cynthia's perfidy, and he didn't believe it would serve any purpose to expose her. The truth would certainly hurt her parents, who were good friends of his parents. He had simply gone into seclusion after her death and let people draw their own conclusions.

*He must have loved her an awful lot to be so torn up.*

*Imagine losing your future bride and your un-
born child at the same time. What a tragedy!*

*It must have been true love. He's been devastated
by her death.*

It wasn't only grief he had felt, it was bitterness,
and a deep and abiding anger. Cynthia's prophetic
words had come true. He would have to live the rest
of his life with the consequences of throwing her out.

In the years after her death he had gone through
women one at a time, testing them and finding them
wanting. Flighty creatures. Dishonest creatures.
Tantalizing, tempting, titillating creatures. He
couldn't keep himself from looking at them with a
jaundiced eye any more than he could keep himself
from needing them to assuage his physical desire.

*So why is a bitter cynic like you marrying a nice
kid like Rebecca Littlewolf?*

Zach heaved a mammoth sigh. What on earth had
possessed him? He wanted to think it was a simple
matter of expedience. He had interviewed enough
women to realize he wasn't going to find the perfect
wife through a newspaper advertisement. But he
hadn't wanted to court a woman because that would
have suggested he wanted affection to be a part of
their relationship. Since he didn't intend to love his
wife, he didn't think it was fair to expect her to love
him.

And Rebecca Littlewolf was a known quantity. He
had been a little surprised at her interest in using his
money to start a camp. But it eased his conscience to

know she had mercenary motives for marrying him. Money he could freely offer. Love was out of the question. It helped that she assumed, like everyone else, that he was still in love with Cynthia Kenyon.

It was an added bonus that he was physically attracted to Rebecca. He had been astonished at his body's instant response to the sight of her when she appeared at his kitchen door. Rebecca only came to his shoulder, but her body curved in all the right places. It was something he had noticed six years ago, although he had refused to act on his interest at the time, in spite of her invitation.

But there was more to like about Rebecca Littlewolf than her body. From the first day he met her, when she was a kid of thirteen, she had worn her heart on her sleeve. It had been a huge heart, for a kid, open to every wounded, needy or crippled being that crossed her path. He wondered how much of that openhearted, guileless girl remained in the woman she had become.

Zach shoved his fingers through his hair in agitation. At least he wouldn't make the same mistakes the second time around. He wouldn't set his heart on a platter for another woman. He refused to make himself vulnerable ever again to the kind of pain Cynthia had caused.

But he desperately wanted children of his own. By the time his thirty-sixth birthday had come and gone, he had realized that time was running out. Conceding that a wife was a necessary part of the family he craved, he had decided on an advertisement as the quickest way to interview the broadest range of candidates. He had been determined to make a rational, informed decision. He had wanted a woman he could admire and respect as the mother of his children, someone with whom he could live amicably. It was icing on the cake if he felt physical desire for her. In Rebecca Littlewolf he had found a woman who filled all his needs.

It took Zach a moment to realize that the soft thumping sound he heard was someone knocking at the back door. He sprinted to the bedroom, dragged on a pair of jeans over his briefs, and buttoned a couple of the buttons as he headed for the kitchen.

The morning sky was streaked with pinks and yellows that gave him enough light to see who was standing there.

"Hello, Zach."

"Come in, kid." As he had the previous day, Zach held the screen door wide for Rebecca Littlewolf. She stepped just inside and stopped.

"I didn't sleep much last night," she said. "I think we need to do some serious talking."

"Uh-oh." Zach hid his anxiety behind a grin, and gestured Rebecca farther into the kitchen. She crossed to the spot she had taken the previous day, in front of the sink. He didn't feel like sitting down, so he leaned against the center island and crossed his arms and his ankles. "What's on your mind?"

She let go of the strand of hair she had tangled around her forefinger and said, "I'm having second thoughts, Zach."

Zach felt a sudden lurch in his belly. He hadn't been particular about who his wife was before he had decided on Rebecca. Suddenly, he couldn't picture anyone else in the role. He found her lowered gaze and tucked chin enchanting. He wanted nothing so much as to lift that chin and kiss those eyelids.

"We shook on it, kid. As far as I'm concerned, it's a done deal."

"It isn't that simple, Zach."

"Why not?"

"Because of Cynthia."

He wondered exactly what she meant and was afraid he knew. "What about Cynthia?"

"I've been wondering whether, for the rest of my life, when you look at me, you'll be seeing her instead."

Zach snorted. "You don't look at all like Cynthia." She blushed a fiery red, and he realized she had taken his comment wrong. Her next words confirmed it.

"I know I'm not beautiful, like Cynthia, but—"

"Looks had nothing to do with my decision," Zach interrupted, unconsciously confirming her opinion that he found her wanting. "Look, kid—"

"I stopped being a kid years ago, Zach."

She shoved her hair behind her shoulders, revealing rounded breasts beneath a worn T-shirt that were proof of her point without the need for words. But he knew she wasn't making reference to her physical maturity. He conceded that he didn't know her as an adult. The woman standing before him was as much a stranger to him as any of the other candidates he had interviewed.

It was disconcerting to admit that he had been calling her "kid" to keep her at a distance. At the same time, he had been using it as a term of endearment. The kid he had known was sweet and kind and had a heart of gold. He wanted to hang on to that memory of goodness as long as he possibly could. He had liked the kid he knew. It was hard to acknowledge those admirable qualities in the sexually attractive woman who stood before him. So "kid" it was ... and would remain.

"All right, kid, let's hear it. What did you decide during your sleepless night?"

She took a deep breath and let it out slowly. "I was thinking maybe it would be better if we didn't get married."

"We had a deal."

"I'm not reneging on the deal, just changing it a little."

His eyes narrowed. "Changing it how?"

"I'm suggesting we live together, rather than marry right away."

"What purpose would that serve?"

"It might save us both a nasty divorce."

"Do you have any reason to believe you can't—or won't—get pregnant?"

She shook her head. "But that doesn't mean it will happen, either."

"I'm willing to take my chances."

"I'm not."

He grimaced. The teenage girl he had known and liked, the one who had marched to the beat of her own drummer with an army of three-legged, lop-eared, crop-tailed animals trailing along behind her, had grown into an equally obstinate and opinionated woman. She was playing with her hair again, which he recognized as a sign of nerves. He wanted to free her hands and take them in his own, to give comfort, to ease her fears.

He took a step toward her, and she extended her hand, the palm flattened in a signal to stop.

"Don't," she said in a breathless voice.

He took another step, and another, until the flat of her palm rested against his chest. Zach stopped then, because he had what he wanted. He could feel the heat of her, feel his heart pound beneath her trembling hand. She looked up at him with eyes that revealed her vulnerability.

She wanted him.

Zach swore under his breath. She had never been good at hiding what she was feeling, and she did nothing to mask the desire that glowed in her eyes. He had seen the look before in other women and knew she was a moment from surrender.

"Don't look at me like that, kid," he warned in a low, husky voice, "unless you mean what you're saying with your eyes."

She jerked her hand away and tucked it behind her. Her eyes blinked several times as though she were recovering from a trance. "I'm sorry, Zach. I didn't mean—"

He laughed, a rumbly sound deep in his chest. He reached out and folded her in his arms, rocking her back and forth several times. "Ah, kid, what am I going to do with you?"

"Why can't we just live together, Zach? I promise I'll marry you when—if—I get pregnant."

He shook his head. "That isn't good enough." He didn't—dared not—trust her. What if she no longer wished to marry him once she was pregnant? At least if they were married he would have some legal right to his child. But he wasn't going to put ideas in her head by mentioning his fears.

"It has to be marriage, kid. I don't want my child born a bastard, or left counting the months between our marriage and his birth."

"Don't you think *our* child is going to ask questions when *she* notices the nature of our relationship?"

"We'll be sleeping together. We'll be civil at the breakfast table. That's more than most marriages can boast," Zach said flatly.

Her brow furrowed. "I don't understand you, Zach."

"You don't have to understand me. That's not part of the job description. All you have to do is keep your part of the bargain."

She turned her back on him and stared out the window over the sink into the central courtyard. "I don't know, Zach."

He closed the distance between them and slipped his arms around her waist. She stiffened, then relaxed against him, into him. He heard her gasp as his palms flattened against her belly, but she didn't fight his intimate possession of her. He lowered his head and nuzzled the soft skin beneath her right ear.

She made a purring sound in her throat that caused his body to go hard. His hand slid down the front zipper placket of her jeans until he was cupping her. She spread her legs and arched into his hand.

"Zach."

A shudder reeled through him when she said his name.

"I... want... you so much." The words seemed forced from her and were followed by a guttural sound of pleasure.

"Marry me," he murmured in her ear. "Marry me and have my baby."

"Oh, Zach, you don't play fair."

His mouth suckled a tender spot on her nape, and she hissed in a breath of air.

Then he felt her hand on his thigh, high up, near his genitals. She wasn't playing too damn fair herself, Zach thought as his blood pumped, and his breath grew ragged. Soon she had both hands behind her, both hands cupping him, and he leaned into the pleasure, reached out for it, groaning in satisfaction at the way she touched him.

"No marriage, Zach. Not until there's a baby."

Abruptly he freed himself. He grabbed her by the shoulders and spun her around. His hands tightened on her shoulders as his eyes flashed with anger. "That sort of blackmail won't work."

He let her go and stepped back. "I have my reasons for wanting marriage first. I'm not willing to compromise, and I'm not going to change my mind. That's the deal. Take it or leave it."

For a terrifying moment, he thought she was going to leave it. She stared at the toe of her booted foot, dragging it back and forth several times across the brick-tiled floor.

"All right, Zach," she said at last. "I think you're making a mistake." Her lips twisted. "I think I'm making an even bigger one. But I'll marry you."

"In two weeks?"

"Two weeks."

"I'll have my lawyer draw up papers to guarantee funding for the camp. We can sign them before the wedding."

"Have your lawyer send them to my lawyer first," Rebecca said.

Zach looked at Rebecca with searching eyes. The kid he remembered would have believed the best of him, not taken precautions against the worst. No, she wasn't a kid anymore, no matter what he chose to call her.

"Fine," he said. "Anything else?"

"What time should I be at the courthouse?"

"Meet me at my lawyer's office at 3:00." He gave her an address. "We'll go from there to the courthouse."

She smiled in a way that was unutterably sad. "I hope neither of us will be sorry a year from now for making this devil's bargain."

"If you're having second thoughts, just don't show up at the courthouse."

Zach was sorry the instant the taunt was out of his mouth. He was no longer willing to settle for just any woman. He wanted Rebecca.

"Goodbye, Zach." She crossed past him without looking back, her shoulders squared and her chin high.

Zach had no idea whether she meant goodbye until the wedding, or farewell forever. He opened his mouth to ask and snapped it shut again. He would burn in hell before he admitted to her that he cared, one way or the other.

For the next two weeks, that's just what he did.

# Three

"Hi, Kid. Are you awake?"

"I am now," Rebecca mumbled, still half asleep. She checked the clock beside the hotel bed. "It's 5:00 a.m., Zach."

"Time to rise and shine, sleepyhead."

"Goodbye, Zach."

"Whoa, kid," he said with a laugh. "I wanted to let you know you're welcome to move your things in this morning. I'll be out working on the range, so you'll have the house to yourself. Kid? Are you there?"

"Sure, Zach. That sounds like a good idea."

"I could hang around if you need any help."

"I loaded the trailer. I can unload it."

"Okay, don't get your dander up. I'll see you later this afternoon, then."

"Goodbye, Zach." Rebecca dropped the phone into the cradle, groaned and shoved herself upright.

Her wedding day had arrived.

Rebecca was no more certain that she was doing the right thing now than she had been two weeks ago. Mrs. Fortunata, however, had been overjoyed.

"See? What did I tell you?" She dabbed at her eyes with a hankie. "I can't believe you want me to be a camp counselor. No more mopping floors! I'm one lucky old lady. That's for sure!"

It had felt good to make Mrs. Fortunata happy.

Rebecca winced at the thought of having to explain to Zach that—without consulting him—she had hired Mrs. Fortunata—and expected him to pay her—to cook for them during the months when camp wasn't in session and—also at his expense—let her live in the counselor's suite in the girl's bunkhouse year-round.

Mrs. Fortunata needed that kind of security in order to leave her job at the hospital. And Rebecca had made up her mind that, once she left the hospital, Mrs. Fortunata was never going to mop or buff another floor in her life.

It vaguely troubled her that she hadn't inquired whether Mrs. Fortunata could cook. However, it had seemed a logical assumption for a woman with that many kids and grandkids. And even though Mrs. Fortunata had never held a position exactly like the one Rebecca had offered her at the camp, Rebecca knew she would be wonderful with the children.

She gnawed on her lower lip. She would just have to tell Zach what she had done at a time when he would be receptive to the idea.

As she drove under the black wrought iron archway that spelled out *Hawk's Pride,* she watched for her first sight of the whitewashed, Spanish-style adobe house that would soon be her home. Wooden posts that served as ceiling beams protruded at intervals along the high walls of the flat-roofed structure. She backed the rented trailer up to the kitchen door, but instead of going inside immediately, followed the stone path that led into the central courtyard.

The house, which was shaped in a square, had been built around a moss-laden live oak that was twice as tall as the roof and which provided a mantle of cooling shade. A latticed arbor near the sliding glass door to Zach's bedroom was draped with fragrant wisteria that hung down above a wooden swing big enough to seat two comfortably. The whole area was bounded by grass and flowers that created a delightful lover's bower. Rebecca couldn't help wondering if Zach had ever made love to Cynthia there.

She forced her thoughts away from Cynthia Kenyon. It would be too easy to let herself get eaten up with jealousy of a dead woman. But her stomach churned at the thought of what mementos of the other woman she might find in the house.

Rebecca let herself into Zach's bedroom through the sliding glass door. The blinds were closed, and it was dark and quiet and cool inside. Zach had a housekeeper several days a week, so there wasn't a speck of dust to be found on the tile floors, but a Western shirt had been thrown over the arm of a wooden rocker, and several ranch magazines lay on the floor beside the unmade four-poster bed. She could still see the imprint where Zach's head had lain on the pillow. From the tossed look of the sheets, he was a restless sleeper.

To her dismay, a picture of Cynthia Kenyon sat on Zach's dresser where he couldn't help but see it each morning when he awoke.

She was tempted to pick up the magazines and make the bed. And remove the photograph from Zach's dresser. She resisted the impulse, but exorcising the ghost of Cynthia Kenyon was high on her list of Things to Do When I Marry Zach.

"Hello? Kid, are you here?"

Rebecca froze when she heard Zach calling to her from the kitchen. She hurried from his bedroom, unwilling to meet him there. She nearly ran into him as they met in the archway to the living room.

"Oh, there you are," he said.

She laughed nervously and sidestepped her way farther into the room, keeping her distance from him. "I thought you planned to be gone from the house."

"I took a break from fence mending on the chance you might need some help lifting boxes after all."

Rebecca looked at him closely for the first time and was struck dumb by what she saw. He had obviously been engaged in hard physical labor. A pair of worn leather gloves stuck out of his back pocket. His plaid Western shirt was open down the front and hanging outside his jeans, and his chest glistened with sweat. His Stetson showed a ring of dampness near the concha band, and the hair at his nape clung to his skin in wet curls. His boots were dusty, his jeans dirty and torn at the knee.

She wanted to touch him, to lay her hands on his slick skin, to taste the salt on his neck, to shove the hat off his head and feel the coolness of his damp hair and the heat of his flesh. She was amazed at the flood of purely sexual desire that made her knees feel weak.

"Zach."

"Oh, kid, don't look at me like that. Not now. Not yet."

Rebecca took a step toward him. She hesitated, remembering the picture of Cynthia in the other room.

*Be careful, Rebecca. Oh, be careful. He's still in love with another woman,* an inner voice cautioned.

But Cynthia was dead. Zach was hers now, and she wanted to touch him. She could tell from the fierce, possessive look in his eyes that he wanted her, too.

She took another step, and another, until only inches separated their bodies. She could feel his heat, smell the musk of hard-working man. She turned her face up to him and waited. Her body quivered with anticipation.

Zach stared at the woman before him. He had dreamed every night of finding her waiting for him like this. The reality slammed him in the gut like a fist. Her body called to his in a way that was as primitive as man himself. His genitals drew up tight, and he felt the blood pounding in his temples. He wanted her like he had never wanted another human being in his life.

Rebecca was helpless to move. She could see the threat of violent passion in Zach's taut face, in his tense body, and noted the flimsy leash by which he had it tethered. Her eyes fell closed in surrender.

His mouth was incredibly gentle when it touched hers. He came back for another touch, another taste, his tongue dipping slightly, then retreating.

She groaned. "More, Zach."

His mouth captured hers in another kiss, powerful with longing, hungry for satisfaction. Suddenly she had what she wanted, his arms crushing her, drawing her close. Her unbound breasts nestled against his hard chest, and she could feel and smell and taste him.

Her hands slid around his neck, and she arched toward him to feel the hardness, the strength of him.

"I have to touch you," he said, his voice raw with need. He ripped her T-shirt up over her head and made a sound of satisfaction when he caught sight of her naked breasts. He stopped for a moment and put her away from him and took his time admiring her.

She fought the flush of embarrassment at standing naked before him, and lost. She crossed her hands over her breasts and struggled to hide the panic she felt. What was she doing? What was she thinking? This was insane. They were going to be married in a few hours.

"Zach, wait. I . . . we . . ." She swallowed hard.

"It's all right, kid. It's only me."

Her glance shot up to meet his dark eyes. His facial muscles were rigid, his jaw clenched, his nostrils flared. But there was something in his eyes beyond the glitter of sexual need. Understanding? She lowered her gaze, confused by the feelings roiling inside her.

"I'm being silly," she admitted in a low voice. She tried for a laugh and failed. She took a deep breath and let it out before she lowered her hands and stood before him in jeans and boots and nothing else. Her body was trembling so badly she thought surely he must have noticed. Her chin came up, and she met his glance for the second time.

His eyes were dark and feral. Dangerous.

She fought the need to flee, to save herself from whatever was to come.

Slowly, reverently, his hands reached out to cup her breasts.

She hissed in a breath as his callused fingertips brushed against her nipples, causing them to peak.

"Incredible," he murmured. "So responsive. So very beautiful."

He lowered his head to suckle her.

Rebecca's knees threatened to buckle, and she grabbed hold of Zach's shoulders. She had never felt anything so exquisite. She thought she was going to faint.

She groaned and pleaded for what she knew not. "Zach, please."

He raised his head, and she saw the raw hunger in his eyes. It frightened her, and at the same time left her feeling exhilarated.

"What is it you want, kid?" he said in a voice harsh with unrequited sexual need.

That was the problem. She didn't know what she wanted.

He started to let go, but she put her hands over his to keep them pressed against her breasts. "Wait, Zach."

She had never seen a man want like this, never imagined the things she would feel. The feminine power. The powerful need.

She was afraid of what was to come. She had never done even this much with a man, and she trembled with expectation and with virginal fear. But there was something greater than the fear. Love. And need.

"I want you, Zach."

An animal sound issued from his throat as he lowered her onto the rug that covered the cool tile floor. He unzipped her jeans and yanked down her underwear before freeing himself. He shoved her knees wide apart and thrust inside her.

"Zach, wait—"

But it was too late. She hadn't realized it would happen so fast. She had underestimated the force of his desire, his hunger to be inside her. He had thought she was experienced and had acted accordingly.

Rebecca cried out sharply as he took her virginity. Zach froze.

He raised himself the full length of his arms, but remained inside her. He looked amazed and confused. "You can't be."

"I'm not...anymore."

"I thought...You're twenty-three!"

"Could we discuss this another time?" She lifted her hips enough to make him groan.

"All right, kid," he said. "We'll talk later."

Rebecca could see the restraint Zach used to keep his need in check as he moved slowly, gently within her. His hand slid down between their bodies to caress her, and his mouth brought frissons of pleasure wherever it roamed.

"Your skin is like velvet," he murmured as his lips caressed her throat. "And your hair...I want to wrap myself up in it and get lost. I think...I think..."

Rebecca didn't want Zach thinking, because his thoughts might stray to another woman. She wanted the hungry sexual partner who had been so anxious to have her that he hadn't even waited to undress himself.

She began to touch him, tentatively at first, seeking places that would arouse his ardor. She tunneled her fingers into the springy curls that covered his chest and happened upon a male nipple that hardened as her fingertips played with it. She loved the feel of his skin, the hard muscle and sinew so different from her softness. She shoved his jeans down below his hips and heard him grunt with surprise and satisfaction as she indulged her curiosity and learned the shape of his lean flanks and buttocks.

When her fingers strayed to the area where his inner thigh joined his belly, he tensed. As she caressed him there, he hissed out a breath of air. When she laid the flat of her hand on him he grabbed her wrist and held her still.

"If you touch me there, I won't be responsible for the consequences," he warned.

Rebecca produced a "cat's got the cream" smile. And touched him there.

He gave a harsh groan and found her mouth with his. His tongue mimicked the thrusts of his body. His hand slipped between them, and Rebecca gasped as his thumb found a spot that was particularly sensitive. Her body tightened and stiffened as she fought the sensations Zach was producing with his hand.

"Let it happen," he murmured in her ear.

"I can't—"

His mouth took hers in a hard kiss, and she fought to catch her breath as her body tensed. Too much was happening. She felt her body slipping from her control, the feelings too intense to bear. She was reaching now for something, arching into Zach's body, her hips thrusting in rhythm with his, her mouth open and sounds coming out that would have appalled her had she not been so helpless to prevent them.

Her tongue met his in a duel of passion, while her hands slid down into the crevice between his legs, driving him over the edge.

She felt the warm spill of his seed inside her as her body clenched and went rigid. She heard his shout of exultation mixed with her own ragged cry of fulfillment. And then she felt his weight, hot and heavy as he relaxed his body onto hers.

Her hands slid around him as his head fell into the niche of her neck and shoulder.

His breath was warm and harsh in her ear, and she felt her own chest heaving with the effort to suck enough air to keep her alive.

"I'm too heavy for you," he said abruptly.

A moment later, he had her tucked against his side on the rug that had bunched beneath them, his leg over hers, their sweat-slick bodies joined from chest to hip, their heads lolling on the cool tile floor.

Rebecca was basking in an afterglow of wonder, when Zach brought her back to unrelenting reality.

"It's time to talk, kid."

"What is there left to say?"

"For a start, it would be interesting to know why you kept your virginity for twenty-three years and then couldn't wait another couple of hours for the wedding."

Rebecca was ashamed to admit the answer to Zach's query. Quite simply, she had been jealous of a dead woman. She played with the black curls that covered his chest, avoiding a response.

Zach wouldn't allow it. He put a forefinger beneath her chin and forced her to meet his eyes. "I'd like an explanation."

"There's a picture of Cynthia in the bedroom," she said in a quiet voice.

Zach stiffened. "And you were staking your claim?"

She peered at him from beneath lowered lashes. "Something like that. Did it work?"

"Cynthia can't compete or complain. She's dead."

"Then you won't mind if I put away that picture on your dresser," she retorted.

"Putting the picture away won't make any difference."

Rebecca felt the knot return to her stomach. It didn't matter whether she removed the photograph because the image of Cynthia would always be with him. So, perhaps it was better to leave it there until Zach was ready to put it away, along with his memories of his first—his only?—love.

Actually, Zach no longer needed the picture of Cynthia to remind him of her perfidy. Images of her face on the last day he had seen her had been permanently graven in his soul. But he used the photo to remind him that a woman couldn't be trusted. Looking at Cynthia every day for the past seven years had reinforced his distrust of women and kept him from letting himself get too deeply involved with one of them.

"Go ahead and get rid of it," Zach said.

"You do it. Whenever you're ready."

"All right."

But Zach didn't jump right up and run to the bedroom, as Rebecca had hoped he would. Instead, he said, "How about a shower?"

"Together?" Rebecca asked, startled—and intrigued—by the suggestion.

"Sure. Why not?" He was on his feet a moment later and pulled her up beside him.

They stripped where they were and walked naked down the hall to Zach's bathroom. Rebecca kept sneaking glances at Zach, admiring his lean flanks, his flat belly, and the genitals resting in a nest of dark curls. As his body hardened in response to her avid gaze, she wondered how on earth he had managed to fit inside her.

He met her incredulous glance and grinned. "If you see anything you especially like, feel free to help yourself."

"I like it all," Rebecca retorted, chagrined that he had caught her gawking. "But a hand wouldn't be very useful without an arm to guide it, and if I took a leg, you might have some trouble walking."

Zach laughed as he pulled her into his arms and nuzzled her throat beneath her ear. "I can see you're going to keep me on my toes, kid."

"Actually, I think I'd like you better flat on your back...with me on top of you."

Rebecca lowered her eyes, amazed at her own audacity.

Zach shot a surprised look in her direction. "Really? I'll be glad to give it a try...after we shower."

Rebecca had never had her hair washed by a lover, and she was amused by Zach's playful antics. Part of the excitement in playing with him was the knowledge that at any moment his touches could become caresses.

When they did, she was stunned by the strength of her response to him. For once she was glad to be so much smaller than Zach. He lifted her legs around his waist as they coupled, easily supporting her for the thrusts that led to the culmination of their desire.

Then they showered all over again. When they were done, he wrapped her in a towel and carried her to his bedroom. He joined her in his mussed-up bed, where they reminded each other in murmurs that they had to get to the lawyer's office by three, then promptly fell asleep.

Rebecca woke feeling warm and safe and realized she was snuggled deep in Zach's embrace. Then the hairs prickled on the back of her neck. She froze, and her heart began to thunder in her breast.

Someone else was in the room.

Rebecca clutched the sheet to her breasts as she sat up. Zach was slower to wake and let the sheets fall where they would as he shoved himself into a sitting position.

"What is it?"

"There's someone in here."

Zach looked around the room, then rose and moved toward the door. He looked out into the hall, then shut the door. He walked to the bathroom and checked, then checked the walk-in closet. He came back and stood before her with his hands on his hips. "There's no one in here but us, kid."

"There is!"

"Want me to check under the bed for green-eyed monsters?"

Rebecca flushed. "I didn't imagine it, Zach. There was someone here." She spotted the picture of Cynthia on the dresser over Zach's shoulder and froze.

Zach turned to look at what had caught her eye. He walked over to the picture, braced his hands against the dresser and dropped his head between his shoulders. "I don't believe in ghosts."

Rebecca leapt from the bed, dragging the sheet along with her. "I don't, either." But she had no other explanation for her strong feeling that there was another presence in the room.

He turned to face her. "You don't need the sheet. There's no one here but me."

Rebecca felt the heat skating up her throat. It was absurd to hide herself from him. He had already seen everything there was to see, and in a matter of hours he would be her husband. And he obviously wasn't shy about his nudity. She stubbornly tightened her hold on the sheet. "I don't usually walk around naked," she said primly.

He grabbed a corner of the sheet and began to tug on it. "I want to see you."

"Not now, Zach," she said in a whispered hiss.

"Why not now?"

Her eyes strayed to the picture on the dresser. The other woman stared back at her.

Zach reached behind him and turned Cynthia's photo around the other way. "Does that help?"

Actually, it did.

Zach kept tugging until he had Rebecca between his legs. He backed her to the edge of the bed, then turned and sat down and pulled her into his lap. "Cynthia was a part of my past. She's no threat to you."

"You're still in love with her," Rebecca accused.

"She's dead."

That didn't change what Rebecca had said. It was probably futile to argue the issue with Zach, but she wasn't willing to concede it, either. "Zach—"

His callused hand surrounded her nape and drew her head toward him so he could cover her mouth with his. She was still in a daze when he said, "Come on, kid. It's time to go get married. If we don't hurry, we'll be late for our own wedding."

It didn't make much sense to argue with that.

# Four

Zach's entire family was waiting for them on the courthouse steps—his parents, his siblings and their spouses and all their children. Rebecca felt a rush of butterflies in her stomach.

"I didn't know your family would be here."

"Couldn't keep them away. Mom and Dad didn't attend either Falcon's or Callen's wedding. I'm the last of the Three Whitelaw Brats to get married, so they sure weren't going to miss this one."

"Hello, Rebecca," Zach's mother said with a warm smile. "It's so good to see you again."

"Glad to see my son has a little sense, anyway,"

Zach's father said as he leaned down to kiss her cheek.

Rebecca found herself figuratively enfolded in the Whitelaw family's embrace. It felt good. It felt wonderful. Here was the family she had missed since her father had died. Here was the warmth and comfort she had been seeking all those years since she had left Hawk's Pride. She slipped her arm through Zach's. A man who came from a family with this much love in it couldn't have forgotten the feeling. He just had to be reminded, and it would all come back to him.

She suddenly felt a whole lot better about getting married. After the afternoon they had spent loving each other, she had every reason to hope their marriage would be successful. If she was lucky, she might already be pregnant.

Rebecca was glad, now that she saw how important this wedding was to Zach's family, that she had dressed for the occasion and insisted that Zach do the same.

She was wearing a soft off-white buckskin ceremonial Indian dress. It had a lovely pattern of colorful beads across the bodice and was fringed along the hem and sleeves. She wore matching knee-high buckskin moccasins. A beaded headband across her brow held her hair in place. The ceremonial dress had been worn by her mother when she was married, and by her grandmother before that, going back several generations. She had cajoled Zach into donning a black Western tailored suit with a white dress shirt, bolo tie and black boots.

Zach slipped a possessive arm around Rebecca's waist and began herding his family into the courthouse. "We might as well get on with it. Day's wasting."

Zach was surprised at the tightness in his chest and the ache in his throat when Judge Smithers began the legal ceremony. It wasn't a real marriage; it was simply a business arrangement. He realized now why Rebecca had seemed anxious at the thought of so much family present.

He was aware of his mother weeping quietly to his left, his father's arm around her shoulder. He could hear Callen and Sam's twins arguing over a doll and Callen's futile whispered attempts to shush them. He saw from the corner of his eye how his brother, Falcon held his wife, Mara and stepdaughter, Susannah close with an arm around each of them, and how Mara cuddled their son, Cody, to her breast. Susannah's leukemia had been in remission for four and a half years now. Six more months and the whole family could breathe a huge sigh of relief that she had made it past the five-year mark and was out of danger.

Having family here made what was happening more real. He had wanted the legal ties, but speaking vows to Rebecca with his mom and dad present made his throat close up tight. The surge of emotions was unexpected and unwelcome. He reminded himself that he wasn't marrying to get a wife, he had merely selected an appropriate mother for his children.

He felt Rebecca's hand trembling in his as he slipped a plain gold band on her finger. It dawned on him that his family was liable to raise quite a ruckus if he ended up having to divorce her in a year.

"You may kiss the bride," Judge Smithers said at last.

Zach caught his breath at the look in Rebecca's eyes when she turned her face up to his. A single diamond teardrop slipped from her eye. Before he could stop himself, he leaned down and kissed the tear away. Then he caught her chin with his hand and tipped her mouth up to his.

He kissed her lightly and released her, afraid to do more than that, afraid to claim her mouth with his, as he felt the strong desire to do. No sense planting any more false hopes in his family than were already rooted there.

"Congratulations, son." His father hugged him hard and then turned to take both of Rebecca's hands in his. "I know you're going to make Zach happy. I hope this marriage turns out as well as those of my other two children have. My best wishes for a long and fruitful life for both of you."

This was getting worse and worse. He watched with alarm as his tearful mother hugged her new daughter-in-law.

"Welcome to the family, Rebecca. I wasn't in favor of Zach's method of choosing a wife, but I'm so pleased that it brought you to him."

"Thank you, Mrs. Whitelaw."

"Please, call me Candy. Or Mom, if you wish."

Rebecca shot him a look of desperation, and Zach recognized her dilemma. To call his mom "Candy" would be to deny the relationship his mother so obviously hoped would develop between them. To call her "Mom" was to set everyone up for greater heartache if the marriage ended in a year.

Zach came to his wife's rescue, slipping his arm around her waist and pulling her snug against his side. "Thanks, Mom," he said, saving Rebecca from having to say anything at all.

"I've got a wedding cake and some supper at Hawk's Way for everybody," his mother said. "Will you and Rebecca come?"

How could he deny the look of entreaty in his mother's eyes? He fought the grimace and managed a crooked smile. "Sure, Mom. Becky and I have to make a stop by the house first, but we'll be there."

To Zach's mortification, his sister had brought rice for everyone to throw on the courthouse steps—only, it was birdseed instead of rice. It wasn't entirely inappropriate to observe that ritual of fertility, he thought. But it was one more indication that his family expected the marriage to thrive and prosper. He hoped and prayed it did.

He grabbed Rebecca's hand and ran for his pickup, dragging her behind, only to discover that Just Married had been scrawled across the back window with shaving cream, and a host of boots and cans had been tied to the back end.

He wanted to laugh and curse at the same time. Didn't they get it? It wasn't real. He had married for convenience. He didn't want all these trappings. They made him uncomfortable and forced him to confront the utter unfairness of the bargain he had made with Rebecca.

From the grim look on her face, she wasn't any more happy with the situation than he was.

Zach heard the shouts of laughter as he picked Rebecca up and practically threw her into the seat of the pickup before running around the hood and letting himself inside. He gunned the engine and peeled rubber as he left the cluster of well-wishers behind.

As soon as he hit the edge of town, he slowed down.

"Is there something you really want from the house, or was that a ploy to avoid your family for a little while longer?"

Zach sighed. "Was it that obvious?"

"It was to me. I don't think your family noticed. They have no idea, do they, Zach, about the truth of our relationship?"

"No."

Rebecca groaned. "I can't possibly call your mother 'Mom' under the circumstances. But I'm afraid otherwise I'll hurt her feelings."

"Then call her 'Mom,'" Zach said irritably.

"What if I don't get pregnant, Zach? What if this all turns out to be a farce?"

"We'll worry about that when the time comes. Right now, we just do what's necessary to get through the day."

Zach stopped at the house, knowing he had to pick something up or have his lie exposed. When he stepped inside the house behind Rebecca, he knew exactly why he would have come straight home if this had really been his wedding day. He caught his wife's wrist and stopped her just inside the kitchen door.

"Hey, kid."

His voice was low and vibrant, and Rebecca felt a shiver of expectation scurry up her spine. She turned as Zach tugged on her hand until she was facing him. His hand caught under her chin and lifted her face until she had no choice except to look at him.

"Hello, wife."

It had a good sound, a marvelous sound. "Hello, Zach." She caught the edge of a frown. Had he expected her to call him husband? She wanted to, desperately. But she had begun to realize that she needed to protect herself if she was going to survive the coming year. Zach had made the rules. She had to follow them. That meant keeping her distance emotionally to the extent it was possible. At least until she was pregnant. Then it would be safe to love him, but not until then.

He made a growling sound in his throat. "Lord, how I want you!"

"Now? But we have to get to Hawk's Way—"

He shook his head. "Not right away. Not for as long as it would take me to love you."

Rebecca felt goose bumps the size of eggs pop up on her arms at the thought of repeating what had happened earlier in the day. "Oh, Zach."

He didn't need more invitation than that.

"Let's get out of these clothes," he said.

Rebecca watched as Zach yanked off his boots, then grabbed for his bolo tie. In moments he was stripped bare. He was already aroused, and she was intimidated by the size of him.

She had dragged her dress off and quickly slipped out of the silk bra and panties that were all she had worn under the buckskin, but Zach was way ahead of her.

"Leave the moccasins on," he said in a sharp voice.

Rebecca froze. She was naked except for the headband and moccasins. Somehow she didn't feel self-conscious, not with the clear look of admiration in Zach's dark eyes.

He fingered the beaded headband and let his hand smooth down the length of her hair to cup her breast. "You look so beautiful...my very own Indian princess."

His eyes were heavy-lidded, his nostrils flared for the scent of her. He reached out and drew her close, sliding her into the cradle of his thighs. He lowered his head and touched his lips to hers.

This time Rebecca knew what to expect, or thought she did. Only, this time, Zach was in no hurry at all. He took his time kissing first one side of her mouth, then the other, before stroking the length of her closed lips with his tongue. She gasped, and his tongue slid inside, warm and wet and demanding.

His hands caressed their way down her back to her buttocks and then between her legs, forcing her to spread them so that he could reach her nether lips. Her knees nearly buckled as he slid a finger inside her. And another. His teeth caught on an earlobe and nipped until the pleasure turned to pain. He soothed the hurt with kisses.

Abruptly, he picked her up and carried her toward the bedroom. Only, to her surprise, he didn't stop there. He shoved open the sliding glass door and stepped out into the sunlight.

The arbor was as beautiful as she had remembered. The air seemed misted with the fragrant scent of wisteria. He laid her down in the cool grass and mantled her body with his own.

She grasped his forearms as he spread her legs with his knees, and gave a startled cry when he thrust inside her to the hilt.

"Are you all right?"

Her blood was racing, her pulse was pounding, but there were flowers overhead and birdsong and sunlight dappled by the giant oak. She was more than all right. "I'm fine, Zach. Oh, I'm very fine."

He slid his hands beneath her and supported her as he made slow, delicious love to her.

Rebecca began to writhe beneath the onslaught of his mouth and body. She returned the favor, nipping at his shoulder, kissing and touching whatever part of him she could reach.

Zach's control didn't last long.

Rebecca was watching his face, so she saw the moment when his eyes closed. He gritted his teeth and then groaned savagely as the pleasure flooded through him.

By then she was no longer watching him. Her eyelids had fallen closed as she threw back her head and gave in to the shudders of intense pleasure racking through her.

They lay together in that lovely bower for long moments afterward. Somehow, Rebecca knew Zach had never been here with Cynthia. For some reason, he hadn't wanted to make love to her in the bedroom. She was glad, because here there was no ghost to intrude on their peace.

"We have to get dressed," Rebecca said when she could breathe easily again. "We have to go to your mother's party."

"I hope you get pregnant soon," he muttered.

Rebecca recoiled. Zach's comment was like a glass of cold water in her face. It reminded her why he had married her, what one use he had for her, and the reason he had been so willing to make love to her. He wanted her pregnant. His expertise as a lover was a benefit to her, but her pleasure was not a primary reason for their coupling.

"I have to get dressed." Her words came out sounding sharper, more barbed, than she had expected.

She stood and felt embarrassed suddenly to be still wearing her moccasins. She turned and fled.

Zach had felt Rebecca stiffen in his arms and wondered what he had done to offend her. He hadn't intended to make love to her in such a frenzy, but once the idea had occurred to him, the need to touch her, to kiss her, to put himself inside her, had been overwhelming.

Instead of taking her to bed, where any sane man would have made love to his brand-new wife, he had carted her outside and laid her in the grass. No wonder she was upset. But he had realized, as he entered the bedroom carrying Rebecca in his arms, that he didn't want to make love for the first time as man and wife in the bed where he had found Cynthia joined with another man.

He turned onto his stomach in the grass and laid his cheek on his folded arms. He hoped Rebecca was already pregnant. He didn't want to get to know her any better—and he admitted he was curious about what kind of person she had turned out to be—until he was certain their relationship would be permanent. His family weren't the only ones who would suffer if there was a divorce. He knew it would be difficult to put experiences like this one behind him and forget Rebecca Littlewolf if she didn't conceive his child.

Zach returned to the house through the kitchen door, because Rebecca had locked the sliding glass door and he didn't want to cause a confrontation if he knocked and she refused to let him in. In the kitchen, he put back on his shirt, pants and boots, but left off his jacket and tie.

He found himself pacing the tiled floor as he waited for Rebecca to appear. He resisted the urge to go see what was taking her so long and called to her instead. "Hey, kid! Are you dressed yet?"

He stopped and stared when she appeared in the kitchen doorway. Her eyes were blotchy, and her nose was red. She had obviously been crying. The headband was gone, and so were the moccasins and the Indian dress, for that matter. She was wearing a simple print cotton summer dress with narrow straps that exposed her shoulders, and sandals that left her legs and feet bare. The dress was fitted to the waist and flared into a full skirt. She had gathered her hair into a ponytail so she looked all of seventeen.

His heart lurched.

It was as though he was seeing her for the first time as she really was. A young woman. Very pretty. Open and honest. When he met her glance, he realized the blind trust, which had been there as recently as this morning, was gone. Her green eyes were wary. Her chin trembled.

"I'm ready," she said in a hoarse voice.

"You've been crying."

"I . . . It's been a hectic day."

"It's not over yet. Are you sure you want to go to my mother's party?"

Her chin came up, and her shoulders squared. "Of course."

She still had gumption, Zach thought. At least that hadn't changed. "Let's go, then."

He stood back and was distressed to see that she shied away as she passed by him. He reached out to stop her. "What's wrong?"

"Nothing."

"I would never hurt you, kid."

She turned and looked at him over her shoulder. Her voice was low and vibrated with feeling. "You already have."

# Five

Rebecca took a sip of coffee that burned her tongue and quickly set down her coffee mug. She glanced at Zach, who sat on the opposite side of the kitchen island. "It's that time of month," she blurted. Meaning, of course, that she wasn't pregnant and that they wouldn't be having intercourse for the next few days.

For the third month since she had married Zach, her period had come exactly on time. She risked a glance at Zach and found his expression as grim-lipped as she had expected it to be. She bit back an apology. It wasn't for want of trying that she wasn't pregnant. She and Zach made love at least once every day and sometimes twice. She had begun to look forward to those interludes, because otherwise, Zach avoided her company.

Her dream of making Zach fall in love with her had gone dreadfully awry. On the other hand, she was making tremendous progress on her camp for kids with cancer, which she had—quite cleverly, she thought—dubbed Camp LittleHawk. Zach had done everything she had asked to help make the camp a reality. Unfortunately, she had yet to fulfill her part of the bargain by providing the child he so desperately wanted.

"Maybe I should go see a doctor," she suggested.

"I think it's a little soon for that, don't you?"

"I don't know what to think," Rebecca replied irritably.

She had discovered that Zach never argued when he could get his way by completely avoiding a discussion of the subject. She watched him do it now.

"I noticed that both bunkhouses are finished," he said. "If I'm not mistaken that means you have everything in place for your camp to open. When does the first bunch of kids arrive?"

"Tomorrow," she said, her face lit by the excitement she felt. "We'll have an even dozen, six boys and six girls."

"I met your new assistant yesterday."

"Rowley? I know he'll be great with the kids. He always has a smile on his face," Rebecca said. "It also turns out that he was raised on a ranch, so he's comfortable around horses and cattle."

"He's got a broken arm," Zach said.

"Well, yes, that's true," Rebecca said. "But he's quite good at saddling horses one-handed."

Rebecca had first spotted Rowley Holiday hitchhiking along the highway into town with a saddle thrown over his shoulder. Of course, she had stopped to pick him up. At first, the young man had been a bit taciturn, but soon she had him talking about his life as a rodeo bronc rider. His broken arm was a bit of bad luck, he said, that was going to make things a little tough for the six weeks it took his arm to heal.

She liked his enthusiasm for his work and his willingness to shoulder life's burdens with a smile. The next thing she knew, she was offering him the job as camp counselor.

Like Mrs. Fortunata, Rowley had no credentials for the job. But it wasn't a conventional kind of camp. Although every child coming to the camp had cancer, they were all in remission or stabilized by treatment. She had arranged to have a doctor on call, but the truth of the matter was, all she needed was a pair of willing hands—or even one good strong one—and an authoritative voice to direct the boys, while she and Mrs. Fortunata took care of the girls.

"It's perfect," she had said. "You can spend some time working for me and Zach and then hit the rodeo circuit again."

"Oh, I don't know, ma'am . . ."

That was another thing she liked about the cowboy, his courtesy. "You have to take the job, Rowley. Camp's starting in a week. I had talked my husband into taking the job, but he's awful busy with ranch business. You'd be doing us a favor.''

And of course, being the nice sort of man he was, Rowley had accepted the job. She had brought him back to the ranch and told him to make himself at home in the counselor's suite in the boys' bunkhouse.

''Is there anybody else you've hired that I should know about?'' Zach asked.

''Nobody since Mr. Tuttle,'' Rebecca said.

''Thank God,'' Zach muttered. ''And about Tuttle—''

Rebecca didn't want to argue with Zach about her newest employee, so she jumped up and dumped the rest of her coffee in the sink. ''I've got to get moving, Zach. I'll see you tonight.''

Zach felt the butterfly touch of her lips on his cheek before Rebecca flitted out the door.

He left the kitchen a moment or two after her, headed for the barn. He watched her fanny sashay across the yard, not quite believing the upheaval in his life since the day three months ago when they had gotten married. It had dawned on him, finally, that Rebecca hadn't changed much at all since the days when she had roamed Hawk's Pride with a menagerie of animals in tow. She was still bringing home strays. Only she had graduated to the two-legged variety.

Besides Mrs. Fortunata, who insisted on cooking for them to pay her way until the first campers showed up—and was a passable cook, if you liked a lot of pasta—there was the cowboy with the broken arm, Rowley Something, whom she had hired as a camp counselor, and an arthritic old man, Mr. Tuttle—who couldn't close his fingers around a pitchfork, let alone lift a bale of hay—whom she had hired to muck out the stalls and feed the dozen-odd ponies she had talked him into buying for the camp.

It wasn't that he couldn't afford the salaries. He had started out with a sizable trust fund and had turned a profit with his ranch over the past fifteen years. He could easily be termed a wealthy man.

"But if you keep it up," he had warned Rebecca, "Hawk's Pride will become a Mecca for every freeloader in Texas with a sob story."

She had looked up at him earnestly and said, "I would never let anyone take advantage of your generosity, Zach."

How was he supposed to respond to a statement like that?

Hog-tied and buffaloed by a bit of female fluff, that's what he was. He had given up trying to stop her from rescuing the homeless, the helpless and the unhealthy. Her generosity of spirit was simply a part of who she was.

Besides, Mrs. Fortunata was a nice old lady, and Rowley had turned out to be a damned hard worker, even with one hand. And somehow, he had no idea how, Mr. Tuttle kept the stable clean and the ponies fed.

Zach watched from the barn, where he was saddling his horse, as Rebecca headed for one of the two bunkhouses—one for boys and one for girls—that had been built to accommodate the twelve pint-size campers. Rowley was working on a corral that would be used as a riding ring for beginners.

Zach pulled the cinch tight and lowered the stirrup but didn't mount immediately. He leaned his arms on the saddle and watched Rebecca talk animatedly with the broken-winged cowboy.

His marriage wasn't turning out at all the way he had expected. In the first place, he hadn't anticipated being so fascinated by his wife. Most of the time, he couldn't keep his eyes off her when they were in the same room together. Only last night, a tiny mole beneath her left ear had drawn his eye and his hand and finally his mouth. At breakfast, he had found himself imagining the feel of the delicate curls at her nape, the curve of her brow. Even this far away, he wasn't immune to her charm. He felt his stomach sift sideways as she gave the new cowhand a sassy smile.

If it had simply been a matter of physical attraction, he might have sated himself with her body long before now. But he had been surprised to discover that he liked Rebecca most when she was discussing her plans for the children who would attend Camp LittleHawk, or the people she encountered who only needed a little helping hand—which she was glad to offer—to get on their feet again. Her eyes laid bare a warmth and enthusiasm for life that drew him like a hot fire on a cold Texas night.

He worried that he might be letting his admiration for her get in the way of his better judgment. This wasn't a real marriage. She wasn't a real wife. Their relationship was supposed to be strictly a business arrangement.

Zach snorted. It never had been that, and he doubted it ever would be.

He felt an urgent need, however, to protect himself from the pain of another failed relationship. He had never seen Rebecca look sideways at another man, so perhaps she would never be guilty of infidelity. But he couldn't help the nagging feeling that he was just one more cripple—one with an emotional handicap, rather than a physical one—that she had chosen to rescue, and that, like the others, once he was on his feet again, she would move on to someone else.

Loving her would leave him vulnerable because she might never learn to love him back. Oh, he would be treated with courtesy and care, thoughtfulness and cheer, but that wasn't the same as being loved—body and heart and soul—was it?

The only way he knew to fight his growing attraction was to keep his distance from her. But every time he drew a figurative line in the sand, she adroitly, even nonchalantly, stepped over it. She was constantly coming to him to ask his advice. Did he think blue or green was a better color for the walls in the boys' bunkhouse? Should she start with ten campers or twelve? What kind of crafts did boys like to do? Did he think the private suite for the counselor in each of the bunkhouses was large enough?

Was it any wonder he felt a little anxious?

To make matters worse, while he wanted a child as much as he ever had, the little boy he imagined now had features and a smile that matched those on Rebecca's face. He hadn't expected it to matter which woman was the mother of his child. Suddenly, it did. He had no idea what he was going to do if Rebecca didn't get pregnant before the year was up.

He heard Rebecca laugh, and the husky, full-throated sound caused the hair on his arms to stand up. His eyes narrowed on Rowley, who stood with his hip angled in a cock-strutting pose and a winning smile plastered on his lips. He watched Rebecca lay a hand on Rowley's shoulder and saw Rowley bend his chestnut-haired head to listen intently to what she had to say. Then Rowley offered his hand to help Rebecca sit on a rail of the corral. Only his hand didn't come away once she was up there. It stayed, resting on her thigh.

Zach felt his stomach cramp. The streak of possessiveness he felt took him by surprise. This wasn't jealousy, it was something much more primeval, the response of a male animal whose claim on its mate is threatened by another male animal. He knew from bitter experience that an unwary man could have his woman stolen away from him.

Adrenaline flowed. Muscles flexed in readiness to fight.

Zach stalked toward the corral, his eyes never leaving the sight of the masculine hand on his wife. He wasn't seeing Rebecca, he was seeing Cynthia in those last moments before he had thrown her out, her body slick with sweat, the sheets tousled around her and musky with the smell of another man. He didn't give Rowley any warning, just grabbed him by the shoulder, turned him around and hit him in the jaw.

"Zach! Are you crazy? What are you doing?" Rebecca scrambled down from the corral and dropped to her knees beside the fallen man. "Are you all right, Rowley?"

Rowley had his good hand to his jaw and was gingerly working it. "I think so." He looked up at Zach. "What the hell was that all about?"

"Keep your hands off my wife."

Rebecca rose and stood toe to toe with Zach. "What's wrong with you? Rowley didn't do anything."

"He was holding hands with you."

"That was perfectly innocent!"

"Yeah. Right," Zach said, his voice harsh with sarcasm.

"I think I'll leave you two alone to work this out," Rowley said, struggling to his feet.

"Don't leave, Rowley," Rebecca said. "Zach owes you an apology."

"Like hell I do."

"Apologize, Zach."

"I'll do better than that." Zach turned to Rowley and said, "You're fired. Pick up your things and be out of here before the end of the day."

Rebecca was furious. "Don't you move an inch, Rowley." She rounded on Zach. "This is my camp, and you have no right to fire my employees."

"This is my ranch, and if I say a man goes, he goes!"

Rebecca shoved a frustrated hand through her hair. "I need him, Zach. I can't manage twelve kids by myself."

"You've got me." It was only then he realized he had been hurt when she replaced him with Rowley. Rationally, he knew she had seen somebody in trouble and been unable to pass him by without offering a helping hand. But it was hard playing second fiddle to another man.

"I know you're there for me, Zach. Lord, I could never face the thought of doing all this without you. But I thought I had put you on the spot asking you to help. We can really use another set of hands."

"He's only got one that works," Zach snarled.

"Nevertheless," Rebecca said, obviously exercising a great deal of restraint, "please tell Rowley you want him to stay."

Zach inspected the cowboy through narrowed eyes. Rowley met his gaze steadily, neither apologetic nor confrontational. It wasn't the look of a guilty man.

So maybe he had gone off half-cocked. Maybe he had acted a little crazy. But Rowley had gotten the point. *Hands off my wife.* As long as that was understood, he was willing to make peace with the other man.

"I'm sorry I hit you," Zach said gruffly.

Rowley took the hand Zach offered. "Forget it, Boss."

"You're welcome to stay."

"Thanks."

"See, now. Was that so hard?" Rebecca said as she slipped her hand through Zach's arm and snuggled close. "I just know you two are going to be great friends."

Zach and Rowley exchanged chagrined expressions. Knowing Rebecca, they probably would.

Zach eyed the eight-year-old boy who stared right back at him with unblinking eyes. "You sure you want to do this?"

"Uh-huh."

He set the boy on top of the small pony and shoved the kid's tennis shoes into the shortened stirrups. He had already given instructions on how to rein the horse. He gave the brim of the boy's baseball cap a tug to make sure it was settled on his head.

All the kids wore caps, he had noticed, because not many of them had hair. Chemotherapy had left them in various stages of baldness.

He met the boy's solemn, gray-eyed gaze and said, "Nothing to it, kid. Let your body move with the horse. If you run into trouble, grab hold of the horn."

"My name is Pete."

"All right, Pete."

Zach mounted his horse and looked back at the line of eight- to twelve-year-old boys mounted on ponies behind him. Rebecca had the six girls mounted in front of them.

"Everybody ready?" He met Rebecca's gaze, and she grinned and nodded.

He heard a chorus of "uh-huhs" and "yeahs" in reply. He noticed Pete, the last in line, was already gripping the horn.

"Let's ride." There were several excited giggles and one "Yippee!"

Zach waited for Rebecca to lead out the girls, then let the boys pass by him before he brought up the rear. He felt a swell of unwelcome emotion at the sight of the kids' faces as they rambled by him. Amazing how a simple thing like a ride on horseback made them so happy.

All except Pete. Pete wasn't smiling, and he had a death grip on the saddle horn.

Zach nudged his horse up beside the boy, who appeared smaller than his age. "You don't have to do this now, if you're not enjoying yourself."

"Yes, I do."

"Why is that?"

"I might not get another chance." He turned and looked Zach in the eye. "You see, I'm going to die."

Zach wasn't sure what to say. He knew Rebecca had medical histories for all the kids, but he wasn't sure whether they included a prognosis for recovery, and even if they had, he hadn't bothered looking at them. He had no idea whether Pete was speaking from knowledge or supposition when he said he was going to die.

"Hell, I mean, heck, we all die someday." Zach glanced guiltily around to see if Rebecca was close enough to hear the profanity he had uttered. He had promised her—crossed his heart—that he wouldn't swear around the kids. It was a hard habit to break. Where Pete was concerned, a little profanity didn't seem out of order.

Zach had never seen such a world-weary, cynical look on the face of a child. The eyes that met his were eight going on eighty.

"I'll be dead before Christmas," Pete said.

"Gosh, I hope not," Zach said.

"Yeah, well, hoping doesn't always help," Pete said.

Zach wasn't sure how much encouragement he should offer. Maybe Pete was right about his fate.

But there were always miracles. He noticed the boy had relaxed in the saddle. "You're doing fine," he said.

"Yeah," Pete conceded. "This isn't as hard as I thought it would be." He shot Zach a self-deprecating smile. "I was afraid I'd get hurt. I sure don't want to end up dying any sooner than I have to."

"I see what you mean," Zach said. "We're falling a little behind. Think you can manage a trot?"

"Sure." Pete grabbed the horn and kicked his mount and quickly caught up to the rest of the kids.

Zach settled back into his position at the tail end of the line. He wished Rowley was doing this job, but the cowboy had stayed at the bunkhouse to organize some crafts for later in the afternoon. Kids like these needed to see a smiling face, and Zach was having a hard time keeping the frown off his.

"I'm taking the canyon trail," Rebecca called back to him.

"All right," Zach said. "Careful you don't end up taking the steep route."

The trail into the canyon forked soon after the descent. One trail was wide and easy to navigate, perfect for the campers. The other was narrow and took a lot of twists and turns. It was easy to miss the turnoff for the first trail and end up on the second.

"Did real Indians draw those pictures?" Pete asked when they passed some etchings on the face of the canyon wall.

"I haven't had an archaeologist out here, but I'd guess so. Some of the artists might even have been my ancestors."

"Or Mrs. Whitelaw's ancestors," Pete chimed in.

Zach raised a brow. "How did you know Mrs. Whitelaw's part Indian?"

"Oh, she told me so when I met her at the hospital."

It had not occurred to Zach that Rebecca might have previously met these children. If he had thought about it at all, he supposed she had passed the word about Camp LittleHawk through doctors who treated children with cancer. But of course she would know any kids who had been patients at Children's Hospital during the past two years.

"How long were you in the hospital?"

"I've been in and out for the past three years."

"You're in remission now, though, right?" It was a condition of attending the camp.

"Yeah. But it's not going to last."

"How do you know."

"I know."

Zach didn't argue. The kid probably knew what he was talking about.

He made an effort to treat the children—many on their first trail ride—as individuals, but he kept seeing them as a group. Without their hair, their faces were hard to distinguish. They all had the same haunted look in their eyes. Some were smiling, some were not. Only their noses were different, pug or pointed or tip-tilted, freckled or tanned.

He wanted to be anywhere other than where he was. It was painful to spend time with these children, to see them experience all this just like healthy children. Because they weren't healthy, and there was nothing he could do to change that. He felt tremendous respect for Rebecca and anyone else who was courageous enough to face sick children every day and pretend that everything was normal. That included his brother Falcon, who had married a woman whose child was deathly ill from leukemia. At least Falcon's stepdaughter was well on the road to recovery.

When they arrived back at the ranch after the ride was over, he made of point of seeking out Pete's records. He had no idea what he would find. What he saw made no sense to him. *Acute myelocytic leukemia.* So, was the kid going to die, or not?

That night, even with his wife safely spooned against his groin and his arm securely around her, he found himself unable to sleep.

"Kid?"

"Umm."

"How could you stand to do it?"

"Do what?" she murmured, already half asleep.

"How did you nurse kids like . . . those kids."

She turned in his arms so she was facing him. He could see the paleness of her skin in the light from the moon that filtered through the open blinds on the sliding glass door, but otherwise her elfin features were masked in shadows. She snuggled her head into the crook between his shoulder and chin.

"You mean, kids with cancer?"

She didn't say "kids who might die" but he knew she understood what he meant. "Yeah."

He felt her shrug.

"You just treat them like kids, Zach."

"But..."

She leaned back, and he could feel her eyes on him in the darkness. "Is it Pete?"

"How did you know?"

"I saw you talking to him."

"I looked up his records. He has *acute myelocytic leukemia*. Is that bad?"

She sighed. "Kids with that kind of leukemia have a very low percentage of survival."

"How long has he been sick?"

"I first met him two years ago. His situation was more promising then. He had acute lymphocytic leukemia, and the disease went into remission. When he relapsed six months ago, he was diagnosed with the more serious cancer."

"He knows he's going to die."

"Most of them have faced that possibility."

"How can they smile? How can they laugh?"

"You mean, how can they keep on living, when life is so uncertain? They don't focus on the past or the future. They live one day at a time."

*Just like me,* Rebecca wanted to say.

"You knew it would be like this," Zach said. It was almost an accusation.

"I knew."

"I didn't believe you, you know."

"Didn't believe what?"

"That you wanted to marry me because of the camp. I thought you made all that stuff up on the spur of the moment."

Rebecca was grateful for the darkness that hid her surprise at his intuitiveness. "Why did you think I wanted to marry you?"

Zach chuckled. "You're going to think I'm an idiot. I believed you were still in love with me."

Rebecca held her breath. *Oh, God. Then why had he married her, if he didn't want a wife who loved him?*

"Now I see it really was the camp you wanted. And I can understand why. It's a good thing you're doing, kid."

"Zach, are you sorry that . . . I don't love you?"

He was silent for a long time. "I think maybe it's better this way. I don't have to feel so guilty, like I'm cheating you, not loving you back. What we have isn't such a bad bargain for either one of us.

"I respect you, and as you pointed out," he said with a grin that showed in the moonlight, "I like you. I can see you'll make a terrific mother. I don't think I could have made a better choice."

She might have confessed the truth, if she had thought it would make a difference. But Zach hadn't said anything about loving her back. She felt like crying and swallowed over the painful lump in her throat.

Zach sought out her mouth in the darkness. She felt his desperation and wondered at its source. She offered him the only comfort she could. Her body melted against his. But there was no lovemaking tonight, not when there was no fertile ground in which to plant his seed.

He pulled her close and held her tight. Gradually his hold on her eased, and his breathing steadied, until finally she could tell he had fallen asleep.

Rebecca was wide awake.

She eased herself out from under Zach's arm and the leg he had thrown over her hip. She silently let herself out through the sliding glass door and wandered barefoot in the grass to the wooden swing, where she settled herself. It creaked slightly as she set it in motion with her foot.

Zach had given her a great deal of food for thought.

*He had thought she loved him. And married her anyway.*

Rebecca wished she knew more about Zach's relationship with Cynthia. The picture that had been in his bedroom the day she moved in still sat on his dresser. It hadn't moved a millimeter in three months. She was as determined now as ever that Zach had to be the one to put it away. But for the first time in months she held out some hope that he would.

# Six

Rebecca was exhausted. She smelled of hay and horses, and it wasn't delicate female perspiration that trickled down between her shoulders but plain old hardworking sweat. She kept glancing over her shoulder at Zach, who was working on the other side of the barn, doing the same job she was, forking hay to the children's ponies.

She had sent Mr. Tuttle into town to buy supplies, insisting that she would rather fork hay than face the crowd at the supermarket. Zach had caught her doing Mr. Tuttle's job and joined her without a word of reproof. She had rewarded him for his forbearance and understanding with a beaming smile of approval. But the whole time they had been working, he hadn't said a word to her. Something was obviously troubling him.

She had a pretty good idea what it was.

Zach had been wearing a frown ever since he said goodbye to Pete. The two of them had spoken only briefly before Pete boarded a chartered plane that was headed back to Dallas with the dozen campers who had completed their week at Camp Little-Hawk. Whatever had been said had obviously upset Zach.

"Want to talk about it?"

Zach didn't answer, just kept forking hay.

Rebecca set her pitchfork against the door to a stall, crossed to Zach and touched him on the shoulder. He whirled at the contact and would have stabbed her with his pitchfork if she hadn't jumped backward. She lost her footing and landed hard enough on the cement floor to elicit a cry of pain.

Zach said a word she hadn't heard all week. He leaned his pitchfork against the wall and stalked over to stand towering over her.

"Are you hurt?"

"My hip..."

He dropped to one knee and with unexpected gentleness began massaging her hip. Rubbing the muscle as he went, he worked his way around to her buttock. "Is that better?"

"Much."

She watched his hand, mesmerized by its strength, by the feelings coursing through her at a touch that wasn't intended to be intimate. Suddenly, all movement stopped. Her glance shot to Zach's face. He was staring at her as though he were seeing her for the first time.

She reached up a hand to brush a curl from his forehead.

He flinched but didn't jerk away. His dark eyes smoldered.

She let her hand drop to her side and lowered her gaze to escape the heat of his. Abruptly, he stood and tugged her to her feet. For a moment she wasn't sure her hip was going to support her. She leaned into Zach and heard him hiss as her breasts came in contact with his chest.

His hands tightened on her wrists to steady her—and to separate their bodies. Once she had her balance, he let her go and took another step back from her. She peeked up at him from beneath lowered lashes.

The frown had become a full-fledged grimace.

Well, it was just too bad if he didn't like being touched. He was in for a lot more touching before she was through. Then she remembered the frown that had been there earlier, the one that had caused her to approach him in the first place. "Zach, is something bothering you?"

He stuck his thumbs in his back pockets. "I don't know what you mean."

"You've had an awful frown on your face ever since you said goodbye to Pete at the airport. Did he say something to upset you?"

Zach gave a snort that was somewhere between derision and disgust. "The kid's dying, and he tells me he's looking forward to seeing me next summer. What was I supposed to say? Yeah, sure, kid, I'll see you next year. If you're still alive!"

Rebecca caught a glimpse of the anguish in Zach's eyes before he turned his face away.

"I can't handle this," he said quietly. "You'll have to hire another hand to help you with the camp. And keep those kids away from me."

He turned to leave the barn. He hadn't taken two steps before Rebecca planted herself in front of him, her fisted hands on her hips.

"Don't you dare walk away from me!"

Zach stopped, but his irritation was apparent. "Don't push me, kid."

"Push *you?* Do you think it's easy for *me* to work with those kids?"

He looked startled. "Isn't it?"

"Heck, no! The first year I was a nurse at Children's Hospital I spent half my time crying. Then I learned that crying didn't change anything. They kept right on dying whether I cried or not. I don't cry anymore, Zach, but the hurting has never stopped. I don't think the hurting ever goes away. But you learn to live with it. You learn to keep on going in spite of it."

Zach shoved a hand through his unruly hair. "So what made you come up with this insane idea for a camp?"

"Is it crazy to want to bring sick kids a little happiness? When I see the smiles on their faces, when I see the shine in their eyes, I feel so good inside that I'm able to deal with the fact that, for some of them, their time is short."

"It doesn't work that way for me. The little bit of joy can't make up for the pain. I quit, kid. Find another fool to do the job." He sneered. "Knowing you, that shouldn't be hard."

Rebecca paled at the insult, but stood her ground. "You can't quit, Zach."

"Watch me."

Zach brushed past her and was nearly to the barn door when one whispered word stopped him.

"Coward."

Zach turned, his eyes narrowed, his face white with furious disbelief. "What did you call me?"

"You heard me. Coward." Her voice was full of the scorn she felt. And the despair. If he didn't learn to deal with the fear of being hurt that was experienced by every person who made a commitment to care, the pain that was always a possibility when one person opened himself to another, his heart was never going to be free to love her. And her marriage was doomed.

"Go ahead, turn your back and leave. Sure, it's easier not to care, but you'll be left with an awfully lonely, terribly empty life. And I won't be a part of it."

Zach reached her in two strides, grabbed hold of her shoulders in a painful grip and shook her until she was dizzy. She knew the exact moment he realized what he was doing, because he stopped so abruptly her chin jerked forward and her teeth snapped together with an audible *snick*.

He released her instantly and stood before her, his chest heaving, his eyes feral, his nostrils flared. A muscle in his jaw spasmed as he gritted his teeth.

"I'm no coward," he said in a low, menacing voice.

"What else do you call a man who won't stand and fight?"

"Fight for what? To watch a lot of kids suffer? Forget it!"

*Fight for us!* she wanted to cry. *For our future together!*

"I guess I should have expected this," she taunted. "It isn't the first time you've turned tail."

"What the hell are you talking about now?"

"I'm talking about Cynthia."

"She's not a fit subject for discussion."

She reached a hand toward him but, much as she craved some connection, didn't actually touch him. She let her eyes caress him as her hands yearned to do.

"You're running from the pain of losing her, Zach. You have been for years. You're so afraid of getting hurt again that you won't let yourself care about anyone. That's why you really advertised for a wife. It was the most impersonal way you could think of to connect with another human being. No danger of caring. No danger of being hurt. Until you stand and face the pain of losing the woman you loved, accept it and move beyond it, you're never going to be over her."

"I'm over her," Zach said bitterly.

"Then why is her picture still sitting on your dresser?"

Zach's mouth opened and shut again before he spoke. "I'm no coward."

"Prove it," she challenged.

"I don't have to prove anything to you or anyone else."

"What about proving something to yourself?"

"I . . ." Zach hesitated.

She set the flat of her hand on his chest near his heart. It was beating frantically. "You can do it, Zach." Her heart leapt to her throat, making it difficult to speak. "Don't quit now."

"Hell, kid. I'll take the damned picture off my dresser."

"That isn't enough, Zach."

"What do you want from me?"

*I want your love.* But there was no way she could tell him that. He had to figure it out for himself. "I want you to keep your promise to help me with the camp this summer."

A callused hand shoved its way through rumpled black hair. "Fine. I'll help with your damned camp. Are you happy now?"

"Yes."

"Can I leave without getting another arrow in the back?"

She managed a crooked smile. "Sure, Zach. I'll go with you. Mrs. Fortunata insisted on fixing supper again. Some kind of pasta, I think. It should be ready about now."

*And I want to see Cynthia's picture—and her memory—finally laid to rest.*

Zach never went near the bedroom until long after his wife had showered and gone to bed. They hadn't made love all week, but she had told him earlier that day, with a blush he had found enchanting, that they could resume lovemaking that evening. After the altercation in the barn, he wondered whether she would let him near her. Not that he had forgiven her for what she had said. There had been just enough truth in her accusation to hurt. But he needed her—the relief of her body, he amended— and he didn't think he could wait another night.

He had postponed going to bed, hoping that she would already be asleep. He had discovered over the past few months that if he kissed her into arousal, when she awoke she wouldn't be thinking of anything except making love to him.

But she wasn't asleep. She was turned on her side facing the doorway, and he could clearly see by the lamp she had left burning on his dresser, that she was awake. Slowly, methodically, he undressed himself until he was naked. He felt her eyes on him, felt the beginnings of arousal. But there was no invitation for him to join her, no sign at all that she would welcome him in bed.

He knew what she was waiting for. She wanted him to put away Cynthia's picture. She wanted him to face the pain of his loss and move past it. Hah! If she only knew! He hated Cynthia Kenyon and always would. Nothing was going to change that. He was glad she was dead.

Except, his firstborn child had died with her. Or maybe she had lied. Maybe it was some other man's bastard.

Zach picked up the picture and noticed his hand was shaking. He crossed to the closet door and opened it and stuck the picture facedown on a high shelf. He stepped back and closed the door. He leaned his forehead against the cool, lacquered wooden surface and held on to the knob for dear life.

He had no explanation for his labored breathing. And the shaking had gotten worse. His whole body was suffused with it.

"Come to bed, Zach."

He couldn't let Rebecca see him like this. He turned to tell her he wasn't ready for bed and saw her arms opened wide to him.

Like a honeybee that sees a particularly spectacular bloom, he was drawn to her. On uncertain legs he made his way the few steps it took him to reach the bed.

There was nothing sexual about the way he crushed her to him. He needed to feel close to another human being, to have the warmth of another body take the chill from his own.

He felt her hands against his face, in his hair, at his nape. Her touch brought fire, and yet the shaking grew worse.

"Oh, my darling. My sweetheart. It's all right. I'm here."

He heard her crooning to him, calling to him, and yet he seemed to sink farther into a deep abyss. He was so cold. He could feel himself shivering with it.

He burrowed his face against her throat, but he needed to be closer still, so he shoved her legs apart with his knees and thrust inside her.

She was warm and wet. He felt himself sinking farther into the well, into pitch blackness. There was nothing now but him and the promise of her.

And the pain.

It was the pain that made him tremble, the pain that sucked at him, drawing him deeper into the gloom.

His body drove into hers as he fought the pull of the darkness. He felt the sharp sting of her fingernails in his shoulders, her heels in his buttocks, dragging him back to the surface. He heard the guttural moans issuing from her throat and smelled the scent of her arousal as he fought his way back to her, to the light.

He felt his body tighten, felt the primitive urge to claim his mate. He could see the light a little way beyond him and fought his way toward it. His lungs heaved to bring him precious air, his body arched as it spasmed, and he cried out into the night as he spilled his seed into her.

He burrowed his head close and squeezed her tightly. He had fought the demons and won. He had found the haven he had sought. She was warmth and brightness. She was life and happiness. She was everything he had ever wanted.

*Don't let yourself be fooled. Remember the pain. Feel the pain. If you feel the pain you won't be vulnerable to the dangerous clutches of love.*

He held on to her, held her so tight he could feel her heart thumping erratically against his own, feel her ragged breath against his throat, feel the slickness of her skin as their sweat-streaked bodies lay intertwined.

"Thank you, Zach," she murmured.

"For what?"

She didn't say anything, and he knew she meant for putting away the picture.

"It doesn't change anything," he said brusquely. "I won't forget her. And I won't fall in love with you."

He felt her tense briefly before she relaxed against him.

"I went into this marriage with my eyes open, Zach. You don't have to keep reminding me how you feel."

But he had to keep reminding himself. It would be so easy to love her. It was so tempting to let down his guard. If he did, disaster was certain to follow. He had to keep reminding himself of that, had to keep himself from loving her.

When he woke the next morning, he looked automatically for the picture of Cynthia. It wasn't there. Like a drug addict, he needed his daily fix of hate and distrust, but it was difficult to manage without a face to focus on. He might have sought out the picture, taken it down from the top shelf of the closet to glance at it, except Rebecca's eyes never left him the entire time he dressed. He wouldn't give her the satisfaction of knowing he had been using the photograph as a crutch.

"I'll go start breakfast," he said at last, conceding defeat.

She crossed to him and slid her arms around his neck and raised herself on tiptoe to find his mouth. Her lips were soft and pliant and tasted like nectar.

"What was that for?" he murmured against her lips.

"Just because."

He read the understanding and approval in her eyes and felt...uncomfortable. He didn't want her feelings about him to matter. Pretty soon he would be doing things just to please her. That sort of behavior led a man down the garden path to danger... to disaster... to love.

"I'll join you in the kitchen in a few minutes, all right?" she said.

"Sure."

Once Zach was gone, Rebecca heaved a huge sigh of... relief... despair... she wasn't sure what.

He had actually done it. He had taken the picture of Cynthia off his dresser and put it away. So why didn't she feel more hopeful about their future together?

It was the desperation she had seen in him, in his lovemaking, that had left her feeling so disconcerted. He must have loved Cynthia even more than she had thought to be so distraught at giving up the chance to look at her picture every day. If he still loved another woman that much seven years after her death, maybe he really wasn't ever going to get over her. Maybe she had been a fool to marry him.

But she couldn't give up now. They had the whole summer ahead of them to work and play together. She was willing to bet that a flesh-and-blood woman could beat the pants off a ghost any day of the week when it came to loving a man.

*He's mine now, Cynthia. Let him go.*

Rebecca shuddered as a draft of cold air wafted across her face. She stopped and stood still as an eerie feeling rolled through her. She looked up and saw she was standing directly under an air-conditioning vent. That had to be the source of the draft. What a silly widgeon she was to imagine Cynthia haunting Zach's bedroom.

She didn't really believe in ghosts, but she couldn't shake the feeling that the other woman was still around. Maybe it had been that picture sitting there all these months. Maybe now she could relax and forget about Cynthia Kenyon.

*There's no need for you to hang around here any longer, Cynthia. Zach belongs to me now.*

The vertical blinds on the sliding glass door rippled.

Rebecca looked up at the air-conditioning vent and gauged the distance to the blinds. She pursed her lips and shook her head.

Naw. She didn't believe in ghosts.

She glanced back one more time at the bare spot on the dresser where Cynthia's picture had stood.

"It's a start, Zach. It's a darn good start."

# Seven

"**I**'m so glad you're home, Zach," Rebecca said. "Sam called, and your sister is in labor."

Rebecca watched the quick grin come and go from her husband's face. He was obviously happy for Callen and Sam, but also reminded by the imminent birth of the Longstreets' third child that after six months of marriage his own wife remained barren.

"I'm sorry, Zach."

"For what?"

"You know what."

"These things take time."

"Half of mine is gone."

"You don't have to remind me." Zach yanked off his Stetson and shoved a hand through sweat-damp hair. "How is that new wrangler working out?"

Rebecca saw how neatly Zach had changed the subject and conceded that perhaps it was better not to discuss what couldn't be changed with words.

"Campbell is wonderful. He doesn't pretend the kids aren't sick, and he's careful to keep an eye out for any problems they might have."

Campbell was a recovering alcoholic who hadn't been able to find a job anywhere in the county to support his wife and six kids. No one trusted him, including Zach, because he had fallen off the wagon so many times. Rebecca hadn't been able to resist his request for a job.

"He's sober now, Zach," she had argued. "And when I think of all those hungry children . . ."

Zach had known he wasn't going to win the debate, but he resisted giving in right away because he liked the methods Rebecca used to cajole him. It had been a pleasure at last to cave in to her entreaties for this latest lost soul.

"All right," he conceded. "Campbell gets one chance. I see him drunk and he's gone."

So far, Campbell had stayed as sober as a Baptist preacher in a dry county.

"At least that's working out," Zach said.

"Yes." Even if their marriage wasn't.

Zach had kept his promise to work with the children, but he hadn't let any of them get close again, not like Pete. He was courteous and helpful, a regular Boy Scout. But he dealt with the possibility of pain by closing himself off from feeling anything. It wasn't the result she had hoped for when she had blackmailed him into working with her the rest of the summer. One more week, and Camp LittleHawk would be done for the season. She didn't hold out much hope that Zach was going to change in the next seven days.

To make matters worse, she had failed to become pregnant. In most marriages, it would be ludicrous to worry that she wasn't pregnant six months after the wedding. With the one-year deadline Zach had set, she was conscious that time was running out.

"I think I have to see a doctor, Zach. At least to give us both some peace of mind."

"That's ridiculous."

Rebecca shook her head. "We know the problem isn't with you. After all, Cynthia was... You can certainly father a child," she finished quickly. "There might be something wrong with me. Something that never showed up during my regular checkups."

Zach closed his eyes. How could he admit to Rebecca that the problem might very well be with him? How could he explain that the child Cynthia carried might not have been his? There was no sense putting her through a bunch of tests if he was the one at fault. But maybe the problem was hers. Maybe it was better to let her be tested first, to make sure of her fertility before he questioned his own.

"All right," he said at last.

He watched Rebecca's shoulders sag as she conceded the necessity for tests. His stomach rolled. He couldn't make her go through that sort of thing by herself. Not when the problem might be his.

"We'll both go," he said.

"What?"

"I said we'll both go."

"But you—"

"Cynthia said the child was mine. There's some question whether it actually was."

She stared at him, her eyes filled with shocked disbelief. "How..."

"The day she died, I caught her in bed with another man."

"But..."

"So we'll both go see the doctor."

Rebecca didn't dare ask the thousand and one questions buzzing around inside her head. The look on Zach's face precluded questions.

"Maybe we'll have a chance to talk to a doctor while we're at the hospital waiting for Callen to deliver," Zach said.

"All right."

Rebecca couldn't quit staring at Zach during the drive to the hospital. He had fooled everybody! His parents, Cynthia's parents, his siblings, even she had believed he had been mourning Cynthia's death all these years. But would a man mourn the death of a woman who had been unfaithful to him? Would he mourn the death of a woman carrying a child he wasn't even sure was his?

*If he hadn't loved Cynthia, what was it that had alienated him from love all these years?*

Rebecca worried her lower lip with her teeth as she reasoned it out. He must have been hurt, humiliated even, by his fiancée's infidelity. No man would be likely to confess the truth.

*So why had he kept Cynthia's picture where he could see it every day?*

To remind him . . . of her betrayal.

Rebecca leaned back against the pickup seat and closed her eyes. She felt like a fool. All this time she had thought Zach was still in love with Cynthia, when he had actually been nursing his hate. Cynthia had torn out his heart and left a deep, vacant hole behind. Zach would never love again, because he had been burned too badly the first time. He would shut her out forever, the way he had shut Pete out when the boy got too close, because he couldn't take the chance that he would be hurt again.

Zach saw the tear slip down Rebecca's cheek and reached out to catch it. As his fingertips brushed her cheek, she leaned into his palm. "I know it must be hard on you to see Callen at a time like this. Especially when you haven't been able...when we... But she expects us to be there. She wouldn't understand why it's painful for us . . ."

"Oh, Zach, you wonderful, foolish man..."

"I suppose we don't have to go, but—"

She scooted across the seat and wrapped her arm around his waist. His arm slid naturally around her shoulders.

"It's fine," she said. "We'll go."

"Are you sure, kid?"

"I'm sure."

Rebecca tried not to breathe too deeply when they entered the hospital, but it was impossible to ignore the smell of disinfectant that permeated the place. In all the time she had worked at Children's Hospital she had never gotten used to it. The astringent smell evoked memories of children she had worked with who had gone home whole and healthy. And children who had not.

She followed a uniformed nurse with her eyes as the woman moved briskly down the narrow green— why were hospitals always beige or green?—corridor.

"Bring back memories?" Zach asked.

She smiled at his perceptiveness. "A few."

"Sorry you quit?"

She shook her head. "I like what I'm doing now a lot better."

"I suppose it beats seeing them sick in bed." Zach precluded her retort by grasping her hand and dragging her onto a crowded elevator. She glared at him, but forbore to argue in front of other people.

Zach held on to Rebecca's hand as a way of allaying his own nervousness. He wanted a child so bad he could taste it. He wanted to see the new baby…and he didn't. He wanted to be happy for his sister and brother-in-law, and yet he was so sick with jealousy that he felt a burning in the pit of his stomach.

It was every bit as painful as he had expected it would be to see the joy in Callen's and Sam's eyes at the birth of their son and know he had no child of his own on the way. It was every bit as difficult as he had known it would be to have the baby thrust into his arms and to feel the softness of its skin, to examine its minute fingernails and lush baby lashes and know the child belonged to someone else.

Worst of all was seeing the look of wonder on Rebecca's face as she held the baby close, to see her flush of embarrassment when the newborn rooted instinctively for her breast as she touched its cheek with her fingertip, and to see the longing in her eyes as she watched Callen nursing her son.

Rebecca looked up suddenly, and their eyes locked. A wealth of words was spoken, though none were said aloud.

*I hope this will be us someday soon.*

Oh, Zach, how I would love to have your child.

*It'll happen. We just have to keep trying.*

What if there's something wrong with me?

*There's nothing wrong with you. You'll see.*

What if it doesn't happen right away?

*We have six months. That's plenty of time.*

I love you, Zach. I've always loved you.

Zach felt the constriction in his chest, a sort of breathlessness caused by what he saw in Rebecca's eyes. She had never spoken of love, not once in all the months they had been married, except to deny it. She had not even said she cared, except for that one lapse when she had called him "darling" and "sweetheart." Only, he wasn't sure he hadn't imagined the words, because he had needed to hear them so badly at the time.

Could he be mistaken about what he saw in her eyes now? Did he want her to love him? Is that why he had projected an emotion where it did not exist?

Of course, she was always touching him. But he figured that was just a habit of hers. She also touched the children often, and the horses and the dog and the barnyard cats. He was no different. Rebecca was a sensual person. If wasn't her fault he reacted the way he did to her friendly pats and affable strokes and inadvertent brushing against him.

He reached out for Rebecca's hand again and, when he had it firmly in his own, said, "We have to be going now."

"Stay a little longer," his sister urged.

"We've got another group of kids, the last campers of the summer, coming tomorrow," Rebecca said by way of explanation for their early departure.

"I should be home in a couple of days. Promise you'll come visit then," Callen urged.

"We will," Zach promised.

"Promise?"

"Promise," Zach said, crossing his heart and holding up three Boy Scout fingers.

He had a death grip on Rebecca's hand and practically dragged her from the room. He wasn't even sure where he was going until he found himself in front of a doctor's door on the first floor in the administration wing of the hospital.

*Dr. Elmo Bently. Obstetrics and Gynecology.*

Zach stopped and turned to stare at Rebecca.

"We don't have to do this now, Zach."

"I think we do."

He knocked and when the doctor called out, he opened the door and pulled her inside.

"What brings you two here?" Dr. Bently asked.

"We want to be tested."

The doctor raised a brow. "Something wrong? One of you sick?"

"For fertility." Zach felt the heat stealing up his throat, but there was nothing he could do to stop it. He pulled Rebecca closer to his side.

The doctor frowned. "Either of you have any reason to suspect you're infertile?"

"Only that my wife hasn't gotten pregnant. And it isn't for want of trying," Zach managed to say.

The doctor chuckled. "Both of you sit down and get comfortable. I think we need to have a little talk."

The doctor asked a series of questions and listened as they answered.

"I'll do some preliminary tests if you insist," he said. "But it seems a bit early to suggest there's a problem with conception. The only possible problem I see is that you may be having intercourse too frequently. The body needs time to recoup, so there may be fewer sperm during subsequent ejaculations. You could try having sex every other day, instead of every day, and see if that helps."

Rebecca wriggled in her seat at such plain speaking. But it was the first encouraging thing she had heard the doctor say. She looked sideways at Zach to see what he thought of this advice.

"All right, Doc, we'll cut back on frequency. But I still want us to be tested. When can we arrange to do that?"

"You can leave a sperm sample now, and I can see your wife in a couple of days."

Zach plainly hadn't anticipated anything happening quite so soon, but he quickly recovered. "The sooner, the better."

Rebecca waited in the hall while a nurse took Zach to another area of the hospital. When it took longer than she expected for Zach to return, she wandered down the hall toward a modern computer information center that listed the location of all the wards. One stood out among the others.

*Pediatrics.*

She took the elevator to the second floor and, when she stepped off, turned away from the nurse's station as though she knew where she was going. In fact, Rebecca knew exactly what she was looking for. Several doors down the hall, she found it.

It wasn't a large room, probably because it wasn't a large hospital. There were eight beds, and each one held a sick child. She hesitated only a moment before stepping inside.

Her eyes were drawn to a girl about five years old. She wore a cast on her right arm and another on her right leg, which was attached to a pulley that kept it elevated. Her face was crisscrossed with tiny scabs that suggested she had probably gone through a car windshield. She was awake, but merely stared at the ceiling.

"Hello," Rebecca said.

The little girl turned big, curious brown eyes on her, but she didn't speak.

"My name is Rebecca. What's yours?"

"Jewel."

"May I sit down, Jewel?"

The little girl nodded.

"How are you feeling?"

"Are you a doctor?"

Rebecca smiled and shook her head. "No, just a visitor."

The girl sighed in relief. "Good. Because I'm tired of doctors."

"Seen too many of them?"

"Uh-huh."

"If you could go anywhere in the world this afternoon, where would you go?" Rebecca asked.

"Home."

Rebecca felt the sting in her nose that preceded tears and blinked quickly to keep them back. She had expected an answer like "Disneyland." How long had this child been here, anyway?

"How long have you been in the hospital, Jewel?"

"A long time."

"I'll bet your mommy and daddy come and visit you a lot."

"My mommy and daddy are dead."

Rebecca brushed a stray curl of plain, Mississippi-mud-brown hair from the girl's forehead while she tried to swallow back the huge lump in her throat. "That's too bad, Jewel."

"I had a brother, but he got killed, too. I just got hurt real bad." Her eyes brimmed with tears. When she blinked, one slid down her too-thin cheek.

"I'm sure someone out there will be glad to have a little girl like you come to live with them. Your grandma and grandpa? Or your aunt and uncle?"

She shook her head sadly. "There's no place for me to go. When I'm well, I have to go to a *father* home, I think it's called."

"A *foster* home," Rebecca corrected.

Rebecca saw the girl's eyes shift upward over her shoulder and turned to see who was there.

It was Zach.

"I wondered where you had gone. I took a wild guess, and lo and behold, here you are."

"I just wanted to visit," Rebecca said.

"Who's your friend?" Zach asked.

"Jewel, this is Zach. Zach, this is Jewel. She's been explaining that she'll be going to a foster home when she's well."

The little girl and the tall man solemnly shook hands.

"Hello, Jewel. It's nice to meet you."

"Hello. Are you a doctor?"

Zach smiled wryly. "No. I'm a rancher."

"Do you have horses on your ranch?"

"Lot of them. Ponies, too."

"I used to have a pony. My daddy and I...my daddy..." The child turned her face away and stared at the wall, clearly overwrought.

Rebecca touched the girl gently on the shoulder and said, "I hope you get well soon, Jewel."

If Zach hadn't taken her hand and pulled her away, she wouldn't have left at all.

Once they were far enough beyond the door that they couldn't be heard, Rebecca turned to Zach, her heart in her eyes. "Zach?"

"I know what you're thinking, and the answer is no."

"She doesn't have anywhere to go. In a week Camp LittleHawk will be done for the season, and it won't be starting again for months. It doesn't have to be forever. A foster home is just an interim step, until someone comes along who wants to adopt her."

"No."

"It isn't as though she's sick. She was injured in an accident. She's obviously well, or nearly well. She will be well."

"No."

"She's all alone in the word, no relatives, nobody. We can't turn our backs on her."

Zach huffed out a breath of air. "There would probably be a ton of paperwork to qualify as a foster home."

Rebecca's grin was blinding. "Oh, thank you, Zach. Thank you. You won't be sorry, I promise you."

"I haven't said yes."

"But you stopped saying no."

Zach chuckled. "You're impossible."

"And you love me for it," Rebecca said with a flirtatious look from beneath long lashes. She realized suddenly what she had said and quickly asked, "How did the test go?"

He couldn't meet her eyes. "First time I've done that since I was a teenager," he muttered.

She couldn't help the giggle that escaped.

Zach picked her up and hugged her tight. "Don't laugh. Your turn is coming."

Both of them sobered at the reminder that they had been unsuccessful in conceiving a child of their own. Zach set her down. "You can pursue the possibility of providing a foster home for Jewel. But be sure you understand we're talking about a temporary situation. If I'd wanted to adopt a kid, I could have done it a long time ago. Don't let yourself get attached to her."

He tipped her chin up to force her to meet his gaze. "Understand?"

"I can care for Jewel without getting emotionally involved. I proved that as a nurse. You don't have to worry about me."

He slid an arm around her waist and headed down the hall toward the elevator.

"Do you think they'll let us have her?" Rebecca asked.

"I think there's a pretty good chance of it."

"What makes you think so?"

"I know the head of social service in town. She owes me a favor for something I did for her in high school."

Rebecca arched a suspicious, inquiring brow. "What, exactly, was it you did for her?"

Zach grinned. "I think that's better left unsaid. Suffice it to say, if you want to foster Jewel, I'll do what I can to grease the wheels."

It was the least he could do. After all, for a welcome change she had consulted him before making a decision about helping somebody. Besides, he was willing to accept the homeless waif on a temporary basis for entirely selfish reasons.

He had discovered, quite by accident, of course, that his happiness depended more and more on Re-

becca's state of mind. When she was sad, he felt bad.
When she was happy, he felt good.

He gazed down into Rebecca's glowing face and
grinned.

At the moment, he felt downright ecstatic.

# Eight

There was nothing physically wrong with either of
them that should prevent conception. That was the
official word from Dr. Bently. But another month
had come and gone, and Rebecca wasn't pregnant.
Thank goodness she had a million and one things to
do to prepare for Jewel's arrival at Hawk's Pride to
keep her mind off her troubles.

She had gone to visit Jewel every day during the
month it had taken to qualify as a foster home and
be assigned to care for the child. She had brought
Zach along several times, arguing that it would help
the little girl to adjust to living at Hawk's Pride if she

knew the two of them better before she left the hospital.

Zach had grumbled, but he had gone.

And had no trouble at all talking with the little girl. In fact, once the two of them got started, it was hard to get a word in edgewise. When she asked Zach about it later, he grinned and said, "I have lots of experience."

Her blank look made him chuckle.

"You forget I've got three nieces. Falcon's daughter, Susannah, comes every year to spend some time with Mom and Dad, and I see her then. Also, I've spent more than a few evenings with Callen and Sam's twins."

Her eyebrows rose.

"In case you're wondering, yes, I've changed my share of diapers and worn the baby powder to prove it. And 'Unca Zach' knows how to play airplane and horsey and motorboat."

Rebecca had laughed at the image he conjured. Then the laughter had choked off, and her heart had leapt to her eyes as she met his gaze. She wanted to see powder on his nose from diapering their child. She wanted to hear a tiny voice calling him "Daddy." She wanted to see him down on his hands and knees in the living room—and be there with him, a giggling child beside them.

She had torn her eyes away from his, because the look of wistful longing she found there was too painful to endure.

She had learned something else about Zach in those early visits with Jewel.

He was mush when Jewel turned those baby brown eyes on him and asked for something. Already the child had gotten him to promise her a pony, and let himself be wrangled into riding with her as soon as she was well enough to do so.

On one of those visits, Rebecca had realized that she was falling in love with Zach all over again. Or maybe it was for the first time.

Her feelings for Zach now were different, stronger, more certain than they had been all those years ago. While she had truly believed she loved Zach when she married him, she had never imagined the depth of feeling a woman could have for a man who cherished her with his body. Or the passion she would experience in the arms of an eager and inventive lover. Or the respect she could feel for a man who was kind and considerate and generous with his time and his money.

But in her wildest dreams, she had never imagined the well of emotion that was tapped when she saw Zach with Jewel. She felt tender and soft, achy and raw. She wanted to give him a child of her body. Her love was a cup that once had been half-full but now was overflowing.

However, the problems in their relationship loomed large.

*Zach didn't love her.*

*Zach would divorce her if she couldn't conceive his child.*

If she let herself think about it too much, she would end up crazy. It was better to live in the present and enjoy her life with Zach as much as she could.

At breakfast this morning, she had reminded Zach to be back by mid-afternoon so they could pick Jewel up at the hospital. She paced the kitchen like a tiger, awaiting his arrival.

The screen door opened, and he stepped inside. "I'm not late, am I?"

She glanced at her watch. "No. I guess I'm just a little anxious."

"You? Nervous? I've watched you face a dozen campers with a grin and a prayer. This is just one little girl."

"But she's going to be ours."

Zach's lips thinned, and his body tensed. "That's not precisely true. We're going to be taking care of her. For a little while."

Rebecca's chin came up. "Maybe so. But while she's in this house, we'll be standing in the role of parents. That's what foster *parenting* is all about. I thought you were committed to having Jewel here at Hawk's Pride, Zach. If you're not, maybe it isn't fair to bring her home with us today."

"I like the kid," Zach confessed. "She's got a lot of guts for somebody that young. I just don't want to set up any false hopes in you—or her—that any of this is going to become permanent.''

''The social service lady already discussed this with Jewel. She understands we're only bringing her here temporarily, that they're looking for someone to adopt her.''

''Poor kid,'' Zach muttered.

Rebecca slipped her arm through Zach's and leaned her head against his shoulder. ''She's going to be fine, Zach.''

''We'd better get going. She'll worry if we're late.''

Jewel was sitting on the edge of her hospital bed waiting for them, her hands pressed between bony knees that poked out from beneath a short plaid skirt. Her face lit up when she saw them.

'' 'Becca! Zach!''

She shoved herself off the bed and gamboled toward them like a filly on newborn legs. It wasn't a graceful trip, because the limp in her right leg gave her an uneven gait. The bone had been broken in so many places that it hadn't mended perfectly. She was always going to have a slight hitch in her step.

Jewel gave Rebecca a quick kiss, then launched herself at Zach, who had no choice except to catch her.

Zach lifted the little girl high enough to make her squeal in mock terror, then settled her on his arm. The scabs were gone from her face now, and only faint pink lines remained. Eventually, even they were supposed to disappear. He couldn't help wondering what the kid's parents had been thinking when they named her Jewel. There was no sapphire or topaz or emerald in her eyes. They were a plain mud brown.

"Ready to go?" he asked.

"You bet! Can we go riding this afternoon?"

"Whoa, pardner! We have to get you settled in at the house first."

"Then can we go riding?" Jewel asked.

Zach laughed. "All right, Miss Persistence. We'll go riding later this afternoon."

"Yippee!"

Rebecca could see why Zach wanted a child so badly. He was a natural-born father. He was completely comfortable with Jewel, and the child responded to his openness by being equally free with him.

Jewel turned to Rebecca as Zach carried her outside and said, "Do I really have a room with a sliding glass door? Our house didn't have sliding glass doors."

As Rebecca buckled the child into the seat belt in the center of the pickup cab, Jewel said, "I can't wait to meet your dog with the raggedy ears. We had a dog, but he ran away and got lost. I always wanted a kitty, but my daddy was 'lergic."

The patter didn't stop. It didn't take Rebecca long to realize that the child was as nervous as she was. In fact, of the three of them, Zach was the least rattled.

Even he wasn't as immune to the excitement of the moment as he apparently wanted her to think. She caught him sneaking glances at Jewel when he didn't think the little girl was looking. He seemed intrigued and entranced by the child's effervescence. Rebecca couldn't help feeling a little envious. She would have given her eyeteeth to catch Zach looking at her like that.

In fact, Zach had been making a mental comparison between Jewel's stubborn determination and Rebecca's insistence on marching to the beat of her own drummer. The two of them—the girl and the woman—were remarkably similar in temperament. Perhaps that was what had drawn Rebecca to Jewel in the first place. Certainly, she had found a kindred spirit.

Once back at the ranch, they only took time for Jewel to change into jeans and boots before they headed for the barn. Jewel had insisted that the three of them ride together.

"I have some chores to do in the house," Rebecca said in an attempt to excuse herself.

"But you have to come! Pretty please?"

"Oh, all right." Rebecca ruffled Jewel's dishwater curls. "But don't think you're always going to get your way just by looking cute."

"That's the pot calling the kettle black," Zach murmured. He had noted with some amusement that Jewel was as good at wrapping Rebecca around her little finger as Rebecca was at manipulating him.

What he hadn't counted on was his inability to say no to the two of them when they ganged up on him.

"I think we should go down the narrow trail," Rebecca said as they approached the canyon.

"Isn't that a little dangerous? Especially for a first ride?" Zach asked.

"I've been watching Jewel, and she's an excellent rider," Rebecca said. "The narrow trail would be more fun."

"Can we?" Jewel pleaded. "Pretty please?"

Zach took one look at the two sets of pleading eyes, one a truly brilliant green, the other an ordinary brown, and gave in. "Just be careful and take it slow. I don't want to have to haul either one of you out of there."

Zach had to admit the narrow, zigzagging trail into the canyon was more fun, and Jewel enjoyed it every bit as much as Rebecca had suggested she would. When they reached the sandy bottom, they set out the simple picnic of ham sandwiches, potato chips and soda that Rebecca had brought along.

Rebecca watched as Jewel automatically handed Zach her bag of chips to open, then did the same with her can of soda. The little girl expected him to be helpful, to be there for her, and he was. Rebecca had to hide her smile when Jewel reached up with her napkin to wipe a dollop of mustard from Zach's mouth.

"Thank you," he said.

"You're welcome," Jewel replied.

Of course, when Rebecca got a little mustard on her lip, Zach didn't do anything as civilized as using a napkin to remove it. He leaned over and thoroughly kissed it off.

Her face was flushed when he released her at last. She was afraid to look and see Jewel's reaction.

To her chagrin, Zach winked at the little girl and said, "Spiciest mustard I ever ate."

Jewel laughed, and Rebecca gave up and joined in.

Jewel became drowsy soon after lunch and settled down on the blanket to nap. As soon as the little girl's eyes drifted closed, Zach pulled Rebecca into his lap and lazily kissed her. His lips played over hers, nipping her lower lip, then sucking on it, then teasing the edge of her mouth with his tongue. His hand closed over her breast, and his thumb brushed the tip, which instantly pebbled.

"Zach, what are you doing?" Rebecca asked breathlessly.

"Can't a man make love to his wife?"

"Not with a little girl sleeping three feet away," Rebecca whispered as she tried to stop his roving hands.

Zach wouldn't be deterred. His hand slid down between her legs to cup the heat of her. Rebecca had never seen him in such a playful mood. It was as though a younger, happier man had taken Zach's place. She wondered what had caused the change, but was afraid to ask for fear of spoiling the moment.

He nuzzled her ear and whispered, "I knew there was a good reason why I married you."

Rebecca looked at him quizzically. "Oh? What was that?"

"I have the hots for your body."

Muffled laughter bubbled from Rebecca's throat.

"And you're going to make an absolutely wonderful mother."

The laughter died. She sought out Zach's eyes. "Do you really think so?"

"Yeah. Anybody with a heart big enough to care for as many strays as you've brought home over the past seven months has to be a good mother."

"Zach...what if I don't get pregnant? What if—"

His fingertips touched her lips to cut her off. "No worrying allowed. We're on a picnic."

He laid her back on the blanket and slipped his hips into the cradle of hers. He rested his weight on his elbows and cupped her face in his hands. He made love to her mouth with exquisite gentleness, drawing out the pleasure, letting it build slowly, but steadily.

She bit back the moans that sought voice, because she didn't want to wake Jewel. Zach teased her and touched her until she was writhing beneath him. He pushed her to higher and higher levels of sensation. She wanted to beg him to stop, because there was no way they could consummate their lovemaking, and they both knew it. But she was enjoying herself too much and, if the hard length pressing against her hip was any indication, so was he.

When they heard Jewel begin to rouse from her nap, Zach bit her earlobe one last time and whispered, "Tonight."

It was an invitation and a promise.

"Tonight," she whispered back.

Of course, neither of them had counted on Jewel having an earache.

They had just put the little girl to bed and slipped under the covers themselves, when they heard a knock on their bedroom door.

Zach quickly pulled on a pair of jeans, cursing when he got them on backward. He barely had them on straight with a couple of buttons done when Rebecca, who had thrown a robe on to cover her nakedness, yanked the door open.

Jewel was standing there in a thin cotton nightgown, her head cocked sideways and her shoulder jammed against her left ear.

"Is something the matter?"

"My ear hurts."

Rebecca dropped down on one knee beside Jewel. She put a hand on the child's forehead. "I think she has a fever."

Zach called Dr. Stephens, the Whitelaw family physician, and got instructions over the phone on what to do to ease Jewel's discomfort. He relayed his instructions to Rebecca, who had already taken Jewel to her room and tucked her back into bed.

"Doc Stephens said if the pain doesn't go away in a couple of hours, or if her fever goes up any more, we need to take her to the emergency room," Zach explained.

"I'll stay with her," Rebecca said. "You go back to bed."

Zach felt awkward leaving Rebecca with the child, but there really wasn't anything more he could do. "I'll check on you in a little while," he promised.

As he made his way down the hall to their bedroom, he heard Rebecca's murmurous voice reading *Winnie the Pooh*.

Zach lay in bed awake—and alone—with nothing to do but think. The bed smelled of the musky perfume he associated with Rebecca, and his groin tightened in a totally natural, if untimely, response to her feminine scent. He told his unruly body to forget it. There wasn't much chance it would be satisfied in the near future.

"I think I've just experienced for the first time what it means to be a parent," he said aloud. He should have resented Jewel's intrusion, but somehow, he didn't. It was instinct, he supposed, the need to ensure the propagation of the species, that caused a parent to subjugate his own needs and desires to that of a defenseless child. It surprised him to realize that he had felt that primitive response to help and protect Jewel, even though she wasn't his own flesh and blood.

"Mother Nature's pretty sneaky," he concluded. He realized he was talking to himself again and shut up.

But it didn't stop him from thinking.

His mind wandered back to the events of the afternoon. He wasn't sure why he had felt so carefree, but he realized now that he hadn't thought once of Cynthia the whole day. That was a new record. The pain and humiliation of that failed relationship seemed very far away. Rebecca made life seem so easy to live. And she was so damned easy to love.

Not that he loved her, of course. Although, it might not be so bad if he did. Except there was a problem that had to be resolved first.

He had given Rebecca a one-year deadline to get pregnant. Seven months of that year were already gone, and the lady was as regular as clockwork.

It wasn't safe to love her yet. Not if he might have to give her up in five months.

*Are you crazy? Give her up? What the hell for? She's a great wife!*

But I want a family, kids of my own.

*Hell, kids grow up and leave you. A wife is forever.*

I can get another wife.

*One as giving as Rebecca? One who'll bring so much marvelous chaos into your life? I doubt it.*

She's not the only woman in the world.

*Face it. She's one in a million. And the lady lights your fire.*

That was certainly true. He had enjoyed himself immensely on the picnic, especially toward the end, when he had been able to hold Rebecca in his arms and make love to her—without actually making love. The slow building of pleasure had been tremendously erotic. He had indulged in touching and tasting to his heart's content. He had felt her shiver of anticipation and known that in the dark privacy of their bedroom later that evening she would finally be his.

Only it hadn't exactly turned out that way.

Zach looked at the clock radio on the bedside table. He had been lying in bed for two hours wide awake. He hadn't heard anything from the other room in quite a while. He dragged his jeans back on and headed down the hall.

He pushed the door open carefully, so as not to wake Jewel if she was sleeping. It took him a moment to realize the bed was empty. His eyes quickly searched the room. The two of them were sound asleep in the wooden rocker in the corner, the child snuggled safe in the woman's arms.

He tiptoed over to the shadowed corner and stood staring down at them. The lamplight glowed on Rebecca's flawless skin, and on Jewel's faint, crisscrossed scars. Jewel's hair was a mass of short curls surrounding her face—such an ordinary brown to be so pretty, he thought. Rebecca's sleek black hair drew his hand, but he resisted the urge to touch, fearing to wake her.

Zach felt a sharp constriction in his chest. His throat closed up, and his nose stung. He couldn't remember the last time he had shed a tear for anyone or anything. But he felt like crying. Because he wanted what he saw, and he knew he would never have it.

Rebecca wasn't going to get pregnant. He wasn't going to be that lucky. He was going to be forced to choose between her and a child of his own. He could see it coming. He had imagined watching his children grow and prosper on Hawk's Pride for so many years, that he fought giving up his dream. He wanted children of his own.

But what if the price for children of his own flesh and blood was giving up Rebecca? Could he return to the empty life he had led before she came to fill it up?

He quietly backed out of the room.

Zach returned to his bedroom and shoved the sliding glass door open so he could hear the night sounds, so he could feel the evening breeze. The leaves of the live oak rustled, but otherwise the night was silent.

He stepped outside and looked up between the gnarled branches of the live oak at the star-filled sky. Generations of Whitelaws had watched those same stars. Maybe some had even stood under this same tree. He wanted to leave a legacy for the future when he was gone. He wanted to know a part of him survived when there were no mortal remains of Zachary Baylor Whitelaw on this earth. Was that so terrible? Was that so selfish?

*Maybe not so terrible or selfish. But stupid, if it means losing Rebecca.*

Zach sighed. It was premature to create problems where none existed. There was no reason why he had to make a decision now. There were months—five months—ahead of him when the situation might resolve itself. All he had to do was wait.

And pray.

# Nine

"We've found a family who wants to adopt Jewel."

"I see," Rebecca replied to the social service worker at the other end of the phone line. "When do they want to meet her?"

"This afternoon, if possible."

"I see."

"Would that be all right, Mrs. Whitelaw?"

"Of course."

"I'll let Mr. and Mrs. Proffit know that you'll be expecting them."

Rebecca set the phone down and turned to Zach, who was sitting at the kitchen island with a cup of coffee in front of him. Jewel was still sleeping.

"That was social service," Rebecca said. "They've found someone who may want to adopt Jewel. Mr. and Mrs. Proffit. They'll be coming to meet her this afternoon."

She sank onto a bar stool and dropped her head into her hands. "Oh, Zach, we've only had her three weeks!"

"This is what's best for Jewel, kid. She needs a mom and dad."

Rebecca's head jerked up. "What's wrong with us? She loves us, Zach. She won't want to leave."

"She's a child. She'll do what she's told."

"She'll be upset. She'll cry."

"She'll get over it."

"How can you be so heartless?" Rebecca demanded.

"I'm being realistic," Zach replied in a steely voice. "You always knew this arrangement was temporary."

"I didn't think they'd find anybody so soon." Rebecca's hands turned white-knuckled as she clenched them before her. "Or that I'd grow to love her so much."

She turned beseeching eyes on Zach. "Can't we keep her, Zach? Please?"

"She's not a lonely old lady or a down-on-his-luck cowboy. She's a growing child. She needs parents who can love her and provide her with a stable home."

"I love her. And if you'd let go of that stubborn pride of yours and admit it, you love her, too," she argued heatedly. "We don't have to let Mr. and Mrs. Proffit take her. We can give her a home, Zach."

"I don't want her!" Zach rose so violently that the stool skidded several feet, tottered and fell with a crash. "I want my own little girl. I—"

A whimper from the doorway cut him off. Zach felt a wrenching tear somewhere inside him when he saw Jewel standing in the doorway to the kitchen. She was still dressed in her nightgown, her hair in tumbled curls around her pinched white face. Her tiny hands were knotted into fists, and her chin trembled.

Good Lord, how much had she heard? Obviously, too much. And not enough. She had no way of knowing that his need for a child of his own had nothing to do with any lack in her. It was a fault in him, a pride of family that had been bred deep, and which he seemed unable to relinquish.

He exchanged a helpless look with Rebecca, whose face was nearly as pale with distress as the child's.

Zach quickly crossed to Jewel and bent down on one knee in front of her. When it appeared the little girl was going to turn and run, he took hold of her shoulders and held her in place.

"Jewel, listen to me."

"No! You don't like me! You don't want me here!"

Zach felt a sort of frantic fluttering inside. "Oh, Jewel, baby, I like you lots and lots. It's just...there are some nice folks who want to adopt you and make you their little girl forever and ever. Rebecca and I—"

"You don't want me." Her chin had sunk all the way to her chest. Her shoulders were slumped. The first tear spilled onto her scarred cheek.

"Oh, sweetheart..." Zach was torn in two. He couldn't say he wanted Jewel without offering hope that he and Rebecca might be willing to adopt her. But he didn't want to adopt her. There was nothing wrong with Jewel; she was a great kid. She just wasn't *his* kid.

He pulled the little girl into his arms and hugged her tight. There were tears in his eyes when he turned to Rebecca, completely frustrated, unsure what logical argument he could use to assuage the painful disillusionment of a five-year-old child.

Rebecca joined the two of them, and Zach opened one arm to pull her close.

"I promise to be good," Jewel sobbed.

"Oh, Jewel, you already *are* good," Rebecca crooned.

Zach couldn't say anything at all. His throat ached, and the muscles refused to work.

"It isn't that we wouldn't love to have you for our very own little girl," Rebecca said, "but..."

She met Zach's eyes, and he could see she wanted him to change his mind. But he had to draw the line somewhere. Otherwise, he was liable to find his house populated by homeless waifs. Jewel was lovable, but so were a lot of other kids. Slightly, but certainly, he shook his head no.

He flinched under the lash of scorn in Rebecca's eyes. It took every ounce of grit he had to hold to his convictions.

Rebecca's voice was calm, soothing, as she spoke to the distraught child. "There's a mommy and daddy coming to visit this afternoon who want you, oh, so badly, to come live with them. Wouldn't you like to meet them?"

"Noooooo," Jewel wailed. "I want to stay here. I don't want to go away. I love you."

She clutched at Zach's neck as she sobbed brokenly.

Zach saw Rebecca draw blood as she bit her lip to hold back her tears. He had to get away, or he was going to give in to them. He thrust Jewel into Rebecca's arms.

"I've got work to do. I'll be back this afternoon before the Proffits arrive."

Even far out on the range, all alone on horse-back, Zach heard Jewel's pitiful voice in his head.

*I don't want to go away. I love you.*

And saw Rebecca's searing look of scorn.

He knew he had disappointed them both. He hadn't been the hero they had hoped for; he had been the villain.

That was the problem with being married to Re-becca. He was always trying to live up to her expec-tations of him. And often failing miserably. Over the past nearly eight months they had been married he had tied himself in knots trying to please her, to win a smile of approval from her. He suffered mightily those times when her glance told him he hadn't measured up.

Like now.

She had wanted a knight in shining armor to come to the rescue. He had acted like the evil magician in-stead, waving his wand to make the child disappear.

The truth was, now that he had some time to think about it, he conceded there was plenty of room at Hawk's Pride for one more. Who said they couldn't keep Jewel and have their own family, too? He had heard of instances where a couple who apparently couldn't conceive a child adopted one and then mi-raculously had their own.

He had learned from watching his brother, Fal-con, that a man could love a child who was no relation to him as much as any father loved his own flesh and blood. It explained the pain he was feeling now at the thought of what his life would be like if Jewel wasn't a part of it. He would always worry whether she was warm and well-fed and happy.

He couldn't wait to get back to the house to tell Rebecca that he had a change of mind. He knew she would be pleased, and he hoped Rebecca and Jewel would forgive him.

He spurred his horse into a gallop and raced across the rugged countryside. Neither he nor his horse saw the rabbit hole until too late, and horse and rider both took a hard fall. Zach lay stunned for a moment, the air knocked out of him. As soon as he could, he rolled over to see how his horse had fared. The animal was back on his feet, but hobbling badly.

Zach shoved himself painfully to his feet and realized he had injured his ankle. He limped over to check his horse. The right foreleg wasn't broken, but the gelding had a bad sprain.

He had stopped swearing since the kids had shown up for camp, because he never knew when one of them was going to be around. But sometimes, nothing else expressed what he felt quite so well. And there were no kids here, at least a dozen miles from the nearest civilization.

"Damn it all to hell!" he muttered viciously.

There was no way he was going to get back to the house before the Proffits arrived. Oh, dear God. What if they took Jewel away with them? Rebecca would never forgive him. He would never forgive himself.

Rebecca was inwardly furious. Not only had Zach left her to handle a distraught five-year-old, but he hadn't returned as he had promised to deal with Mr. and Mrs. Proffit.

She greeted the couple cordially at the door. "Hello, Mr. and Mrs. Proffit, I'm Rebecca Whitelaw."

"Please, call us Dan and Susan," Dan said as the couple stepped inside.

They looked like very nice people, Rebecca thought. Dan was dressed in an expensive suit and tie, and Susan was wearing a designer dress and nylons. They were a little older than she had expected, maybe their middle thirties, but both of them were very attractive, what some might call "beautiful people."

"I thought Jewel would be here," Susan said.

"She's in her room. I hoped we might talk for a few moments first." She had no power to deny Dan and Susan if they wanted to adopt Jewel. Nevertheless, she felt a responsibility to ascertain what kind of parents they might be.

"Do you have other children?" Rebecca asked.

"No. We've tried, but we can't have children of our own," Susan said.

"I'm sorry." Rebecca had more empathy for their situation than she was willing to reveal. "Have you been trying to adopt for very long?" She had heard there were lengthy waits to find a child.

"We've only been looking for a year," Dan said.

Rebecca frowned. It sounded like they were shopping for a used car. "Would you like me to tell you a little about Jewel?"

"We'd rather meet her and make our own judgment about her," Dan replied.

"All right. Let me go get her."

Jewel was playing quietly in her room. She had been unusually, extraordinarily quiet ever since Zach had left the house. It was as though by being quiet she might blend into the woodwork, as though, by becoming invisible, Rebecca might somehow forget she was there and let her stay.

"Jewel, the Proffits are here. They'd like to meet you."

"Do I have to?"

Rebecca nodded. She held out her hand, and Jewel gripped it very tightly. When they arrived in the living room, Jewel wouldn't let go, so Rebecca walked past the Proffits, who were sitting on the leather couch, and settled herself in the pine rocker with Jewel standing between her jean-clad legs.

Before Rebecca could even make an introduction, Susan said, "She limps."

"And her face is scarred," Dan added.

"Jewel was in a car accident. That's how she lost her family."

"They didn't tell us about the limp," Susan said.

"Or the scars," Dan added.

"Will she ever walk normally?" Susan asked.

"She walks fine now," Rebecca replied between stiff lips.

"But she *limps!*" Susan exclaimed.

Rebecca felt Jewel stiffen. She circled Jewel's waist with her arm, to offer a bastion of comfort against the verbal onslaught of these rude, insensitive people.

"Will the scars go away?" Dan asked.

"They're hardly noticeable now," Rebecca managed to grit out. "In time they should fade until they're almost invisible."

"Almost?" Dan said, a frown on his face. He exchanged a look with his wife.

Rebecca felt sick. They *were* shopping for a child just like they would for a used car. And they didn't want one with any dents in the fender or scratches on the hood.

The couple rose abruptly. "I'm sorry we wasted your time," Dan said.

"Jewel isn't the right child for us," Susan said.

Rebecca couldn't believe her ears, couldn't believe they were saying these things in front of Jewel, as though she were made of chrome and steel and couldn't hear them perfectly well with her very human ears. She felt incensed at their cruelty.

Rebecca rose like an avenging angel and protectively shoved Jewel behind her. Before she could begin her tirade, she heard Jewel run from the room.

"Jewel, wait—" she called. But the little girl was gone. A moment later Rebecca heard the screen door slam in the kitchen. Most likely Jewel was headed for the barn. She would catch up to her as soon as she finished with the Proffits, and try to undo some of the damage that had been done.

"You two don't deserve to have a child as wonderful as Jewel," she said fiercely. "She might limp, and she might have a few scars on her face, but that child has more love in her little finger than either one of you will ever know. Get out of my house. Get off this ranch. Get out of town. Because by the time I get through giving social services an earful, you won't find a child to adopt anywhere in this county!"

Rebecca didn't wait for them to leave before she headed toward the back door. When she got to the barn she was distressed to see that Jewel's pony was gone. The little girl couldn't heft the saddle, and it was still in place on the side of the stall. But she was perfectly capable of bridling her own horse and riding bareback, and indeed, the pony's bridle was gone.

There were dozens of ways a little girl could get hurt or lost on a ranch as big as Hawk's Pride. Rebecca didn't even have a clue where to start looking.

"Oh, Zach, where are you when I need you most?"

Zach was tired, hot, and hungry when he finally came limping down the dirt road to the main house. He had planted young live oaks the entire distance from the arched entry to the house when he first graded the road, and they provided welcome shade. He could see in his mind's eye the day when the approach to Hawk's Pride would be every bit as impressive as the magnolia-lined drive leading to Hawk's Way.

For the past several miles he had been composing his speech of apology to Rebecca and Jewel. He only hoped he wasn't too late.

Much as he desperately wanted to know how the interview with the Proffits had turned out, Zach headed for the barn first. Any cowboy worth his salt made sure his horse was taken care of before he attended to personal business. It was a habit bred in the

West, because a man without a horse on the vast Texas plains could die walking to water. It behooved a cowboy, even in this day and age, to make sure his horse stayed healthy.

Zach had already unsaddled the gelding when a cowboy entered the barn. Zach started at the sight of the stranger, then realized it was Smitty, the man who had shown up on their back doorstep two days ago. And his newest employee.

He could remember thinking at the time that it was a good thing he had opened the kitchen door to the quiet knock instead of Rebecca. Because he took one look at the cowboy, at his worn boots and frayed jeans and dusty hat, and knew that Rebecca would have hired the man on the spot.

"Can I help you?" he had asked.

"I'm looking for a job."

"I don't need any hands right now." Which was the truth.

"I'm a hard worker."

"I don't doubt it. What put you out of work?"

"Oh. Well." A flush cheated up the cowboy's throat. "The boss and I didn't get along."

"I see." Probably a troublemaker, Zach thought. And felt relieved again that it hadn't been Rebecca who had answered the door.

"Man kicked his dog," the grizzled cowboy said. "Even a dog don't deserve that."

Zach had to agree. So maybe the cowboy wasn't a troublemaker. "I wish I could help you, I just don't need any more hands right now." Especially with Camp LittleHawk disbanded for the summer. In fact, Rowley Holiday had taken off to join the rodeo circuit again.

"I'd be willin' to do just about anythin'."

Zach shoved his thumbs in his back pockets to resist the temptation to hire the man. "I just don't have any work," he said.

The man turned away, hesitated, then turned back. He rubbed his whiskery jaw, then swiped his hand nervously along the leg of his pants. "You see, I got me a sick missus. Cancer. She's in the hospital gettin' chemicals pumped into her right now. I gotta have work to pay the bills."

Zach was certain he could have shut the door with a clear conscience if the man had mentioned any disease except cancer. He had a niece he had watched fight cancer, and he had spent the summer with kids ravaged by the disease. He told himself, when he offered Smitty a job, that he was doing it out of plain Christian charity, not because Rebecca had gotten him to thinking about how he had plenty and enough to share. Or because he knew how pleased and proud she would be of him for making "the right" decision.

In fact, when Rebecca heard what he had done, she gave him a look so tender, a kiss so sweet, that he flushed like a teenage kid asking for condoms at the drugstore.

His decision was vindicated now, because he needed someone to take care of his horse so he could get to the house, and here was Smitty available to help.

"Can I give you a hand, Boss?" the bewhiskered cowboy asked.

"Know anything about sprains."

"Sure do. Worked once upon a time at a racing stable. Got a poultice that'll do wonders. You just leave this cow pony to me. I'll take care of him.

"You better put some ice on that ankle of yours, too, Boss," Smitty said.

"I'll do that. By the way," Zach said as casually as he could, "have you seen Rebecca this afternoon?"

"Yeah. She was headed toward the canyon on horseback."

"Was Jewel with her?"

"Naw. She was alone."

Zach headed for the house. Maybe Rebecca had left him a note. Maybe there was some good reason why she and Jewel hadn't gone riding together. Maybe Jewel had gone over to play with Callen's girls.

*And maybe the Proffits took her away.*

Zach felt a chill of alarm when he entered the kitchen. It was so quiet you could hear nightfall coming. He let the screen door slam behind him and heard it echo through the house.

"Rebecca? Jewel?"

He limped his way down the hall to Jewel's room, afraid of what he would find. His heart was thumping crazily in his chest by the time he reached her doorway.

He made an audible sound of relief when he saw that her things were still there. He crossed to a chest and pulled the drawer open just to make sure. Her tiny T-shirts and flowered underwear were still there. Her favorite doll and her Pooh bear lay on the bed.

So where was she? And why wasn't Rebecca back from her ride? It was nearly dusk.

He headed back to the kitchen, grabbed the wall phone and called his sister.

"Hi, Callen."

"Hello, stranger. We haven't seen you guys since the Labor Day picnic. When are you going to bring Jewel and come visit?"

Zach felt his heart drop to his boots. He knew it was futile, but he asked anyway. "Jewel isn't there?"

"No. Don't tell me you've misplaced the child, Zach. That's a little careless even for you."

"Uh . . . I'm not exactly sure where she is. There were some people here this afternoon who wanted to adopt her."

"I know. Rebecca called me right after you left this morning. How did the interview go?"

"I don't know. I wasn't here."

Callen took an outraged breath, but Zach cut her off at the pass. "Before you start yelling at me, you should know my horse went down in a rabbit hole. The two of us had to limp our way back. I just got home a little while ago."

"Are you all right?"

"I'm fine. I just . . . I can't find Rebecca or Jewel." He shoved a frustrated hand through his hair.

"Shall I send Sam over to help you look?"

"I'll take a portable phone with me, and if I don't find Rebecca where Smitty said she was headed, I'll give you a call."

"All right. We'll wait to hear from you."

Zach wasn't truly alarmed yet. There was probably some perfectly logical reason why Rebecca wasn't back yet. And Jewel might be visiting some other friend. She might even be with his parents.

He had the phone in his hand dialing his parents' number when the screen door screeched open.

He turned with his mouth open to chastise Rebecca for not leaving him a note and froze.

Jewel stood in the doorway. Her forehead was scraped and oozed blood, her face was dirty and streaked with tears. Her lower lip was swollen almost twice its size.

"'Becca," she sobbed. "'Becca."

Zach was across the room in two strides and swept the little girl up into his arms.

"Where's Rebecca?" he demanded.

Jewel clenched his neck so hard she threatened to strangle him. "I'm so-or-ry. I'm so-or-ry," she sobbed. "Po-o-or 'Bec-c-ca."

Zach resisted the urge to shake her. The child was already hysterical, and violence was only going to make things worse. But he was terrified. Sorry for what? Why *poor* 'Becca? Where the hell was his wife? What had happened to the two of them?

Zach did his best to comfort Jewel, but he was shaking so hard himself it took him a long time, too long, to calm the little girl enough so she could speak coherently.

"Where is she, Jewel? Where's Rebecca?"

Jewel's chin trembled. Her mud-brown eyes sparkled with unshed tears.

"Jewel, please, where is she? You have to tell me. I have to go help her."

"You can't help her," Jewel said.

"Why not?"

"'Cause she's dead."

# Ten

Zach's heart missed a beat. His brain denied the words Jewel had spoken. The little girl had to be mistaken.

He set her on her feet and knelt beside her. "You have to take me to her, Jewel. Can you find your way back to where she is?"

"Her horse saw a snake and started bucking. She fell a long way down. I called to her and called to her, but she didn't answer me. I tried to get to her, but the trail doesn't go that way."

He brushed the curls away from Jewel's injured forehead. "How did you get so banged up?"

"Oh. My pony bucked me off, too, but I didn't fall into the canyon."

Zach could see it all, the two horses frantic with fear and with no room to maneuver away from the snake on that narrow, treacherous trail. Rebecca falling . . . falling. How far was "a long way down"? Maybe she was only injured. Maybe she had only been knocked unconscious. Maybe even now she was walking back to Hawk's Pride, wondering where the hell—heck—he was.

"You were a brave little girl to find your way back here all by yourself."

Tears welled in Jewel's eyes, and she shook her head. "I just got on my pony and told him to go home. He's the one who knew the way."

"Still—"

The child clutched handfuls of his jeans leg. "It's all my fault 'Becca got hurt. She told me I shouldn't have run away. She told me she would never have let those awful Poppet people take me away. But you said you didn't want me, and they didn't want me, either—cause I limp and I have scars—and I was afraid."

Zach dragged Jewel up into his arms and hugged her tight. "Oh, Jewel." How could anyone not want her? He knew now what her parents had been thinking when they named her. She was a jewel, all right, one more precious than sapphires or topazes or emeralds. And he would always treasure her as the priceless, irreplaceable gem she was.

It took him a moment to get hold of himself.

"We have to go find Rebecca," he said past the bullfrog-size lump in his throat. "Will you help me?"

"I'll try. What if I can't remember where she is?"

"Don't worry," Zach reassured her. "We'll find her."

He left the kitchen on the run, bellowing for help at the top of his lungs. People came on the fly from all directions.

"Rebecca's been injured somewhere in the canyon. I need someone to call 911 and get the paramedics on the way. Tell them we may need to airlift her from the canyon." If her back was broken. Or her neck.

"I'll do that," Mrs. Fortunata volunteered.

"I need someone to hook the horse trailer up to my pickup and load my horse and another for whoever comes with me. We'll drive to the canyon and go down on horseback."

"I'm on my way, Boss," Smitty said.

"I need someone to come with me to help..." He couldn't make himself say "carry her body," and said instead, "to help me climb down the canyon wall."

"I'll come," Campbell said.

Zach hurried back inside to doctor Jewel's wounds and wait for the call from Smitty that the trailer was ready.

The closer they got to the canyon, the more frightened Zach felt. What if Rebecca was dead? What if he never had a chance to tell her he loved her? Oh, dear God how he loved her! He had been pretending she was just like any other woman, that she could be replaced, because he was frightened of committing himself.

But there was no one quite like Rebecca. No one else would have dared to invade his house with her darling imps and homeless waifs...and make it feel so much like a home.

She had to be alive.

The trip down into the canyon was accomplished as quickly as was humanly possible within the bounds of safety. Zach had taken Jewel up behind him on his mount, and Campbell followed them. They were fighting time, because daylight was fast receding.

When they turned a bend, Jewel pointed down and shrieked, "There she is! Zach, I see her!"

She wasn't moving. Even from where he was, Zach could see blood on her shirt. He gauged whether it would help if they went farther down the trail before he tried climbing down into the canyon, but it bent in the other direction. He was going to have to go down from here to reach her.

He quickly lifted Jewel down, then dismounted and began rigging a rope to the horn of his saddle. He had done enough climbing on these canyon walls as a kid to know what he was doing. He quickly rappelled down the cliff wall, landing not far from Rebecca's body.

As he approached, she moaned.

He fought a gust of totally inappropriate, very relieved laughter. She was alive! That was all that mattered. He bent down beside her, looking before he touched to see the extent of her injuries.

"Kid," he said softly, "you've really done it this time."

To his amazement, she opened her eyes and stared right at him. "Zach. I love you."

His throat ached. He knew why she had said it. Because she thought she was going to die. What a fraud she was, almost as bad as he was. "I love you, too," he said in a rusty-gate voice.

"You do?"

"Yep. Now shut up so I can see how badly you're hurt and get you out of here."

"Is Jewel all right?"

"Jewel's fine. She made it all the way back to the ranch by herself." He didn't think now was the time to tell her Jewel had thought she was dead. "Can you move your arms and legs?"

"Uh-huh. But I think my right wrist snapped when I used it to break my fall."

Her wrist was swollen to twice its normal size. "It looks broken, all right." He examined the cut on her forehead, which seemed to be the source of most of the blood. The head wound was less worrisome, now that he saw she was lucid. He looked at her eyes for signs of concussion, but didn't see any.

"Were you knocked out?"

"I must have been. It was early afternoon when I fell. The next time I opened my eyes, the sun was headed down past the rim of the canyon."

Zach took off his hat, shoved a hand through his hair, and pulled the Stetson snugly down. "I have to decide whether to move you myself or wait for the paramedics."

Rebecca struggled to sit up. "I can—" She winced and grabbed at her stomach.

"Something hurts?" Zach reached around her to support her back.

"I don't know. I must have bounced off a couple of rocks on the way down," she said with a half-hearted laugh. "Feels a little tender."

"Let me take a look." He undid her belt, unzipped her jeans and pulled the tails of her shirt up to take a look at her belly. It was horribly bruised.

"Looks a little beat up." He touched her to see how tender she was, and she cried out with pain.

This looked serious, like maybe she was bleeding internally. Suddenly, the relief he had been feeling that she wasn't paralyzed or concussed vanished. She could die of injuries on the inside, injuries he couldn't see.

He took the time to wrap a bandage around her head to stop the bleeding from the cut there. Then he said, "If you think you could stand it, I'd like to rig a sling to get you out of here."

"Anything," she said. "I just want to go home."

"You're going straight to the hospital," Zach said. "And no arguments."

It was a sign of how bad her injuries were that she didn't make a fuss. In fact, in the thirty minutes or so it took him to get her up onto the trail, her condition deteriorated. She was unconscious again.

"Is she dead?" Jewel asked.

"No. In fact, I talked to her. She asked about you, and I told her how you came home to get help."

Jewel laid a palm on Rebecca's pale cheek and looked up at him. "Is she going to be okay?"

"She's going to be fine. We have to get her to the hospital, though, so they can make her well."

He had to get to the rim of the canyon for his cellular phone to work, but Zach had already decided that Rebecca needed to be airlifted to the hospital. It was the hardest thing he had ever done to watch the helicopter lift off without him.

It took too long to get the horses loaded back up, to drive back to the ranch, and then disconnect the trailer from his pickup so he could head for the hospital.

"Can I come?" Jewel asked.

"No, you have to wait here with Mrs. Fortunata."

"But 'Becca needs me!"

"You can go visit her when she's better," Zach promised.

"But she might die! Like my mommy and daddy died!"

"A hospital is no place for children," Zach snapped, his patience gone. "I have to go. Be a good girl, and go find Mrs. Fortunata."

He turned his back and headed for the cab of the truck. He didn't see Jewel climb into the back of his pickup and hide under a tarp.

Zach parked the truck in the hospital lot and hadn't gone two steps when he felt a small hand insinuate itself between his fingers.

He grabbed hold and turned to find himself staring at a mulish expression every bit as stubborn as anything he had ever seen on Rebecca's face. "How the hell—heck—did you get here? Damn—darn it, Jewel, what am I going to do with you?"

"I *have* to see 'Becca."

Zach didn't have time to take her home now. Grim-lipped, he tightened his hold on her hand and dragged her along with him. "You can sit in the waiting room. But I don't want to hear a peep out of you. Understand?"

"Uh-huh."

Once inside, Zach headed for the closest desk with someone behind it.

"Your wife is in the operating room," the admitting nurse told him. "She had internal injuries that required surgery. The surgeon will come see you when he's finished. There's a waiting room on the second floor."

Jewel was as good as her word. She was quiet as a mouse. But she never left his side, and she was with him every step he took. When he insisted that she stop tagging along behind him, she sat in a chair in the corner and followed him with her eyes. It was as though he was her last connection to Rebecca, and if she let go, she would lose everything.

He understood how she felt.

Zach was surprised when Callen and Sam arrived, although he shouldn't have been. Word passed quickly on a country grapevine. His family had always rallied to each other in times of trouble. His mother and father arrived shortly thereafter, and he had a call from Falcon, asking about Rebecca's condition.

"I don't know anything yet," Zach said. "They're still operating."

"Are you all right?" Falcon asked.

Zach remembered another time, years ago, when he had gone to the hospital with Falcon when his stepdaughter, Susannah, had become very ill, and they had feared it was a relapse of her leukemia. He had wanted to stay and provide a comforting shoulder for his brother. Now he realized why Falcon had sent him away. If he had that shoulder available, he might very well cry on it. And he couldn't afford to fall apart. He had to stay strong for Rebecca. And for Jewel.

"I'll be fine," Zach said. "As soon as I know Rebecca's going to be all right."

"Ask Mom to give me a call when you know something. We'll be praying for you."

"Thanks, Falcon."

It was late when the doctor finally arrived, his surgical greens dotted with dark patches of sweat. Zach recognized him as a guy who had been a couple of years behind him in high school. If he just thought a minute, he would remember the doctor's name. Only his brain was a little jumbled right now. He just couldn't think.

A volunteer had come in and turned off several of the lights, so the room was basked in shadows. Sam and Callen had gone home to put their children to bed, and his parents had retreated to the hospital cafeteria for a quick cup of coffee. Jewel, who had refused to leave with Sam and Callen, and Zach were alone in the waiting room.

When the surgeon approached Zach, his expression was grim. Zach's knees threatened to give way, but he wanted to be standing when he heard what he could see was going to be bad news. "Ted Slocum," the doctor said, holding out his hand.

Zach took it. "I'm Zach—"

"I know who you are, Mr. Whitelaw."

Zach didn't even realize Jewel had joined him until he felt her tiny hand close around his. He gripped her fingers and found as much comfort as he gave.

"Is she . . . How is she?" Zach asked.

"She had serious internal injuries. We couldn't stop the bleeding."

All the blood drained from Zach's face. "She's not—"

"She's alive," the doctor hurried to reassure him.

"Thank God." Zach's eyes closed momentarily in relief. "Oh, thank God for that."

"Her condition is stable, and I expect her to make a complete recovery. But I had to take out her spleen. And her uterus."

It took a moment for the doctor's words to sink in.

*No. Oh, no. Poor Rebecca. Oh, poor Rebecca.*
Zach felt numb, but he knew the pain wasn't far off.
It was like the time he had been stomped by a
Brahma in a college rodeo. For a moment he had
simply lain breathless in the dirt. Then he had tried
to draw air into his lungs, and a fierce, searing pain
had cut across his chest. He fought off the moment
when he would be forced to confront the reality of
the doctor's pronouncement, the moment when the
pain would start.

"We wanted a family, you know. Three kids, or
maybe four. Now you're telling me Rebecca can
never have any children. It's..." He felt his self-
control disappearing as a blinding rage took hold of
him. "It isn't fair, goddamn it! This just can't be
happening. Rebecca will... She... Rebecca... Oh,
God, how will I ever tell her?"

"I'm sorry, Zach. There was nothing else I could
do." The surgeon reached out a hand in comfort, but
Zach shrank away from his touch. The doctor turned
and headed for the door.

"When can I see her?" Zach called after him.

"She'll be in recovery for a while. I'll have a nurse
send for you when she's conscious."

Zach sank into the nearest chair and dropped his
head into his hands. He bit his lip to hold back the
wounded cry that sought voice, but the awful,

wrenching sound escaped his throat and echoed in the room.

He realized now the choice had been made long ago. He could not give up Rebecca. That did not keep him from grieving the loss of his never-to-be-born children. Or the loss of the children Rebecca would have loved the way she loved all helpless living creatures who crossed her path. A tight band gripped his chest making it nearly impossible to draw breath. The emotional pain of this catastrophic event was every bit as bad as the physical pain had been all those years ago.

Two tiny booted feet appeared beside him. He felt a hand patting his shoulder in comfort.

Jewel leaned close to his ear and said, "Don't cry, Zach. 'Becca's gonna be okay. The doctor said so."

He lifted his head from his hands unaware of the tears on his cheeks. "I know, Jewel. It's just..." She was too young to understand the devastation he felt at the doctor's other news.

"Are you sad 'cause 'Becca can't have any babies?"

He had underestimated her. Again.

"Yes, I am."

She played with a frayed spot at the knee of his jeans where it had gotten caught on some barbed wire. Her hand stilled and she looked up at him. "If you want, I could be your little girl."

Zach felt a rush of emotion. How vulnerable she looked, waiting for his answer, her heart right there in those wonderful, unforgettable mud-brown eyes.

He swallowed past the thickness in his throat. "I'd like very much for you to be my daughter, Jewel."

Her gap-toothed smile was slow in coming, as though she couldn't quite believe her ears. Then she launched herself into his open arms, which closed around her.

"Oh, 'Becca will be so glad!" she said. "She told me not to worry, that she'd give you a good talking to, and that you'd change your mind," she admitted with youthful naïveté. "Only you changed your mind all by yourself!"

Zach smiled ruefully and let himself bask in the little girl's grin of approval. Oh, Jewel was her mother's daughter, all right. He was going to have his hands—and his heart—full with the pair of them. Thank God.

Zach surreptitiously swiped the tears from his eyes when he spotted his parents returning to the waiting room. "The doctor's been here, and Rebecca's going to be fine," he said.

"Only she can't have any babies," Jewel piped up.

Zach saw the look of shock and sympathy in his parents' eyes and knew he couldn't stay and talk with them right now. He wanted—needed—to see Rebecca.

"Will you keep an eye on Jewel? I'm going to see Rebecca." He didn't wait for an answer. As the waiting room door closed behind him, he heard Jewel saying, "I'm going to be Zach and 'Becca's little girl."

He smiled. That ought to keep his parents busy for a while.

Zach got directions from a nurse to the private room where they had moved Rebecca. There was a light at the head of the hospital bed that illuminated her face, but the rest of the room was cloaked in shadow. Her eyes were closed, but they opened when he sat down next to her on the bed.

"Hello, kid," he said.

"Hello, Zach."

"How do you feel?"

"Like a horse kicked me in the stomach."

She reached down to her stomach and gingerly touched it. She frowned as she felt the staples in her skin that the doctor had used to close after surgery. "Zach?"

He reached for her hand and brought her knuckles up to his lips. "The doctor had to do a little surgery."

"How little?"

"He took out your spleen."

She heaved a sigh of relief. "Oh, is that all? I think I can do without that."

"And your uterus," he said in a quiet voice.

She snatched her hand from his and winced at the pain caused by the jerky movement. "What did you say?"

"Your life was at stake. The doctor had no choice. He had to remove your uterus." It hurt, oh, how it hurt to see the stricken look on her face.

"No!" she cried. "It's not fair. Oh, Zach, it isn't fair! I wanted to give you children. I wanted—"

He pulled her awkwardly into his arms, trying not to hurt her as he maneuvered her head against his shoulder. He kissed away the hot tears spilling from her eyes. "It doesn't matter, kid. It doesn't matter to me. I'm just so glad you're alive. I love you so much—"

"But—"

"Nothing else is as important to me as you are."

"But—"

"I don't know how I would go on living if anything happened to you."

"But—"

"I love you—"

Rebecca clamped a hand over Zach's mouth. With every word he had said her heart had lightened. It was a blow to realize she could never bear children, but she was more concerned now with what that information meant to Zach. "You said we would get a divorce if I wasn't pregnant in a year. Are you saying you've changed your mind?''

She removed her hand to let him speak.

The silly man nodded vigorously and said, ''Uh-huh.''

Her eyes narrowed. ''You only married me to have a mother for your children.''

''Uh-huh.''

''But I can't have any children now.''

He shook his head. ''Not true. In fact, if I'm not mistaken, you've already got one.''

She stared at him a moment before understanding dawned. ''Jewel? Oh, Zach, are you really willing to adopt Jewel?''

''The kid insists on staying. I couldn't very well throw her out, could I?''

Rebecca smiled through her tears. ''Oh, Zach... We'll have a houseful of kids, I promise.''

''I'd bet on it,'' he said with a chuckle. ''I'd be a fool not to bet on it! I could make a fortune betting on it.''

She laughed, and he lowered his head to capture her laughter with his lips. It was like coming home. His heart thumped a little faster. He might have lost this chance at happiness. He was reaching out now with both hands to love and life. And children. His and Rebecca's children. He wondered who they were, where they were right now, and by what mysterious means they would find their way to his doorstep.

"How many, Zach?"

"What?"

"How many can we have?"

"Oh, Lord," he said with a groan. He should have seen this coming. "Four. Altogether. Not one kid more, Rebecca. I swear I can't handle more than that."

"All right, Zach. Four."

Zach eyed her suspiciously, then shook his head in resignation and pulled his wife close. It was going to be more. He would bet on it. He could make a fortune betting on it. And he would likely need the fortune to feed everybody.

Zach grinned.

"What's so funny?" Rebecca asked.

"I'm just happy." Zach pulled her close. "I'm just a very happy man."

# Epilogue

Seven. Zach hadn't imagined being the father of seven children after ten years of marriage, but he was surviving the experience amazingly well. Jewel was fifteen now, and blessed with two sisters and four brothers. Only one of the children had been a newborn when they adopted him. Colt was seven now and hell on wheels. You weren't supposed to have favorites, but he would always have a special fondness for Jewel, who was the first child to steal his heart, and for Colt, who had known no other father before him.

The other children had all been older when he and Rebecca adopted them, but they were equally precious to him. The other two girls, Frannie and Rolleen, were nine and seventeen now. The other three boys, Rabbit and Jake and Avery, were eight and twelve and thirteen, respectively. Of course, Rabbit's name wasn't really Rabbit, it was Louis. But they had discovered he loved raw carrots and lettuce and all sorts of vegetables, so Jewel had given him the nickname, and it had stuck.

Fortunately, they had a lot of help. Mrs. Fortunata and Mr. Tuttle had fallen in love and married years ago, and the two of them were like another set of grandparents for the children. Thanks to Rebecca, there were always extra hands around the ranch. Some of the Camp LittleHawk kids had even come back to work at the camp and become friends.

Like Pete. Who had beaten all the odds. He was eighteen now and had been a camp counselor last summer. He was heading to college in the fall. He wanted to be a paleontologist, of all things. He said it was the Indian drawings in the canyon at Hawk's Pride that had gotten him interested in the subject.

Zach watched Rebecca edge through the sliding glass door and step into the courtyard.

"Why are you sitting out here all alone in the dark?" she asked.

"It's quiet out here." Which a houseful of kids was not. Ever. Zach opened his arms, and Rebecca settled in his lap on the wooden swing and snuggled her head against his chest. "I was just thinking what a lucky man I am," he said.

"We are lucky, aren't we?"

"Umm." With so many kids, it wasn't always easy to find a private moment with his wife, so he relished this one. He shoved the hair back from her nape and kissed the softness there. She still lit his fire, all these years later, and he felt the slight tension in his genitals as he took the weight of her breasts in his palms.

Rebecca made a kittenish sound in her throat. "You aren't sorry, are you, Zach?"

He was too busy kissing her throat to answer.

"About having so many children, I mean, and not any of them your own."

He raised his head abruptly and dropped his hands from her breasts. He turned her so he could take her face between his palms. He was irritated at having to stop his lovemaking to settle something that he had thought was settled long ago.

"Let's get this straight once and for all. These children are all mine, legally, morally, and every other way. I love them all. I'd give my life for each and every one of them. They're Whitelaws, through and through.

"And I bless the day you came into my life and became my wife. I won't say living with you is easy, because it isn't. There are times I don't think I can be the man you expect me to be, but I keep trying because I love you.

"Which isn't always easy. Because it isn't natural for me to be as open and generous as you are. And sometimes there are so many strangers working around here, it's hard to know who's who.

"But I wouldn't give up one single frustrating, exhilarating, mind-boggling minute of the past ten years."

"Oh, Zach, I'm so glad you feel that way." She fiddled with the collar of his Western shirt. "Because, there's this girl—"

"No. Absolutely not."

"But you just said—"

"Seven is enough. We agreed when your brought Rabbit home that he was the last. I'm forty-six, Rebecca. Forty-six-year-old men don't go around having kids."

"But Cherry is fourteen, Zach. She won't be any trouble at all. Or, maybe only a little."

Zach groaned.

"It seems she has this attitude problem and has been skipping school. Her foster parents finally gave up on her. She's in a juvenile detention center right now, but if we—"

"All right."

"—agree to be her—"

"I said all right."

Rebecca threw her arms around Zach's neck and kissed him all over his face. "Oh, Zach, thank you so much."

Rebecca opened the first two snaps on his shirt and slipped her hand inside to rest it against his chest. "You have the biggest heart of any man I know. And I love you, very, very much."

Eight wasn't so many, Zach thought. But this was absolutely the last one.

Next time he was putting his foot down.

\* \* \* \* \*

**SILHOUETTE®** *Desire* *Hearts of Stone*

Three strong-willed Texas siblings whose rock-hard protective walls are about to come tumblin' down!

The Silhouette Desire miniseries by

**BARBARA McCAULEY**

continues with

August 1995

**TEXAS TEMPTATION** (Silhouette Desire #948)
Jared Stone had lived with a desperate guilt. Now he had a shot to make everything right again—until the one woman he couldn't have became the only woman he wanted.

Then read the conclusion in December 1995 with:

**TEXAS PRIDE** (Silhouette Desire #971)
Raised with a couple of overprotective brothers, Jessica Stone *hated* to be told what to do. So when her sexy new foreman started trying to run her life, Jessica's pride said she had to put a stop to it. But her heart said something *entirely* different....

And if you missed **TEXAS HEAT** (Silhouette Desire #917), the first book in the *Hearts of Stone* trilogy, be sure to order your copy today!

Rugged rancher Jake Stone had just found out that he had a long-lost half sister—and he was determined to get to know her. Problem was, her legal guardian and aunt, sultry Savannah Roberts, was intent on keeping him at arm's length.

HOS2

**He's Too Hot To Handle...but she can take a little heat.**

SILHOUETTE

*Summer Sizzlers*

This summer don't be left in the cold, join Silhouette for the hottest Summer Sizzlers collection. The perfect summer read, on the beach or while vacationing, Summer Sizzlers features sexy heroes who are "Too Hot To Handle." This collection of three new stories is written by bestselling authors Mary Lynn Baxter, Ann Major and Laura Parker.

Available this July wherever Silhouette books are sold.

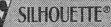

Three brothers...
Three proud, strong men who live—and love—by

**THE CODE OF THE WEST**

Meet Lucas Tanner, one of the Tanner brothers,
in Anne McAllister's

**COWBOYS DON'T QUIT
(D #944, 8/95)**

Luke Tanner was a cowboy through and through.
Now, the rugged landscape was the only thing
keeping the past at bay. Until his past came riding
back into his life—in the form of Jill Crane, the
woman he's never forgotten....

And be sure to watch for Noah's story in
COWBOYS DON'T STAY, coming in
December 1995!

Only from

SILHOUETTE® *Desire*

COW1

# FLYAWAY VACATION SWEEPSTAKES!

This month's destination:

## Glamorous LAS VEGAS!

Are you the lucky person who will win a free trip to Las Vegas? Think how much fun it would be to visit world-famous casinos... to see star-studded shows...to enjoy round-the-clock action in the city that never sleeps!

The facing page contains two Official Entry Coupons, as does each of the other books you received this shipment. Complete and return all the entry coupons— **the more times you enter, the better your chances of winning!**

Then keep your fingers crossed, because you'll find out by August 15, 1995 if you're the winner! If you are, here's what you'll get:

- Round-trip airfare for two to exciting Las Vegas!
- 4 days/3 nights at a fabulous first-class hotel!
- $500.00 pocket money for meals and entertainment!

Remember: The more times you enter, the better your chances of winning!*

*NO PURCHASE OR OBLIGATION TO CONTINUE BEING A SUBSCRIBER NECESSARY TO ENTER. SEE REVERSE SIDE OF ANY ENTRY COUPON FOR ALTERNATIVE MEANS OF ENTRY.

VLV KAL

# FLYAWAY VACATION
## SWEEPSTAKES
### OFFICIAL ENTRY COUPON

This entry must be received by: JULY 30, 1995
This month's winner will be notified by: AUGUST 15, 1995
Trip must be taken between: SEPTEMBER 30, 1995-SEPTEMBER 30, 1996

**YES,** I want to win a vacation for two in Las Vegas. I understand the prize includes round-trip airfare, first-class hotel and $500.00 spending money. Please let me know if I'm the winner!

Name_____

Address _____ Apt. _____

City                State/Prov.              Zip/Postal Code

Account #_____

Return entry with invoice in reply envelope.

© 1995 HARLEQUIN ENTERPRISES LTD.                    CLV KAL

---

# FLYAWAY VACATION
## SWEEPSTAKES
### OFFICIAL ENTRY COUPON

This entry must be received by: JULY 30, 1995
This month's winner will be notified by: AUGUST 15, 1995
Trip must be taken between: SEPTEMBER 30, 1995-SEPTEMBER 30, 1996

**YES,** I want to win a vacation for two in Las Vegas. I understand the prize includes round-trip airfare, first-class hotel and $500.00 spending money. Please let me know if I'm the winner!

Name_____

Address _____ Apt. _____

City                State/Prov.              Zip/Postal Code

Account #_____

Return entry with invoice in reply envelope.

© 1995 HARLEQUIN ENTERPRISES LTD.                    CLV KAL

# OFFICIAL RULES

## FLYAWAY VACATION SWEEPSTAKES 3449

### NO PURCHASE OR OBLIGATION NECESSARY

Three Harlequin Reader Service 1995 shipments will contain respectively, coupons for entry into three different prize drawings, one for a trip for two to San Francisco, another for a trip for two to Las Vegas and the third for a trip for two to Orlando, Florida. To enter any drawing using an Entry Coupon, simply complete and mail according to directions.

There is no obligation to continue using the Reader Service to enter and be eligible for any prize drawing. You may also enter any drawing by hand printing the words "Flyaway Vacation," your name and address on a 3"x5" card and the destination of the prize you wish that entry to be considered for (i.e., San Francisco trip, Las Vegas trip or Orlando trip). Send your 3"x5" entries via first-class mail (limit: one entry per envelope) to: Flyaway Vacation Sweepstakes 3449, c/o Prize Destination you wish that entry to be considered for, P.O. Box 1315, Buffalo, NY 14269-1315, USA or P.O. Box 610, Fort Erie, Ontario L2A 5X3, Canada.

To be eligible for the San Francisco trip, entries must be received by 5/30/95; for the Las Vegas trip, 7/30/95; and for the Orlando trip, 9/30/95.

Winners will be determined in random drawings conducted under the supervision of D.L. Blair, Inc., an independent judging organization whose decisions are final, from among all eligible entries received for that drawing. San Francisco trip prize includes round-trip airfare for two, 4-day/3-night weekend accommodations at a first-class hotel, and $500 in cash (trip must be taken between 7/30/95—7/30/96, approximate prize value—$3,500); Las Vegas trip includes round-trip airfare for two, 4-day/3-night weekend accommodations at a first-class hotel, and $500 in cash (trip must be taken between 9/30/95—9/30/96, approximate prize value—$3,500); Orlando trip includes round-trip airfare for two, 4-day/3-night weekend accommodations at a first-class hotel, and $500 in cash (trip must be taken between 11/30/95—11/30/96, approximate prize value—$3,500). All travelers must sign and return a Release of Liability prior to travel. Hotel accommodations and flights are subject to accommodation and schedule availability. Sweepstakes open to residents of the U.S. (except Puerto Rico) and Canada, 18 years of age or older. Employees and immediate family members of Harlequin Enterprises, Ltd., D.L. Blair, Inc., their affiliates, subsidiaries and all other agencies, entities and persons connected with the use, marketing or conduct of this sweepstakes are not eligible. Odds of winning a prize are dependent upon the number of eligible entries received for that drawing. Prize drawing and winner notification for each drawing will occur no later than 15 days after deadline for entry eligibility for that drawing. Limit: one prize to an individual, family or organization. All applicable laws and regulations apply. Sweepstakes offer void wherever prohibited by law. Any litigation within the province of Quebec respecting the conduct and awarding of the prizes in this sweepstakes must be submitted to the Regies des loteries et Courses du Quebec. In order to win a prize, residents of Canada will be required to correctly answer a time-limited arithmetical skill-testing question. Value of prizes are in U.S. currency.

Winners will be obligated to sign and return an Affidavit of Eligibility within 30 days of notification. In the event of noncompliance within this time period, prize may not be awarded. If any prize or prize notification is returned as undeliverable, that prize will not be awarded. By acceptance of a prize, winner consents to use of his/her name, photograph or other likeness for purposes of advertising, trade and promotion on behalf of Harlequin Enterprises, Ltd., without further compensation, unless prohibited by law.

For the names of prizewinners (available after 12/31/95), send a self-addressed, stamped envelope to: Flyaway Vacation Sweepstakes 3449 Winners, P.O. Box 4200, Blair, NE 68009.

RVC KAL